MW01482898

Praise for Mia Kerick and her books

"Mia Kerick's writing is engaging and perfectly balanced."
Suki Fleet

"Mia's books should be made compulsory reading in high schools."
Mandy Ryder

"The best young adult book I've read, and frankly, this ranks right up there among the best books I've read, period!"
Wendy Ann - "The Red Sheet"

"I think somewhere in the beautiful heart of this author lives a seventeen year old boy.... Authentic, natural, with the angst and anxiety and glorious passions of that age."
Dianne Hartsock

"Mia Kerick welcome to my OMG shelf. Ms. Kerick does a brilliant job of gathering characters from very different walks of life and injecting them with unique voices that give her characters a rich sense of authenticity."
Mel

"What a story. What a wonderful, beautiful story."
Breann - "Us Three"

"I don't read young adult stories all that much, but it is stories like this one that make me willing to try."
Carissa - "Us Three"

Love Spell

Mia Kerick

Young Dudes PUBLISHING

Love Spell

ISBN
ISBN-13: 978-1511831857
ISBN-10: 1511831855

Dedication

To Demi
for always listening

Read this first, hun.

I've been accused of thinking too much, which might be true, but I consider that fact to be a minor blip on my personality radar. Nothing more.

I mean, it's not hurting anybody, is it?

People may call the activity of my mind overthinking, and it wouldn't be a monster stretch for them to call it obsessing. Then, of course, there are those uptight douches who'd slap a neon pink Post-It Note on my brain—the phrase "has a few dozen screws loose" scribbled on it with a chisel tip purple Sharpie.

I, however, choose to view the slightly convoluted manner in which I process thoughts as ingenious. And to be real, at this very moment I have about fifteen more ingenious adjectives, fully capable of describing the way I think, burning a hole in the cargo pocket of my painted-on pastel camo skinny jeans. But I very rarely subscribe to the concept "less is more", and this is one of those extremely rare occasions.

(SMH) Not that I'm happy about it.

In any case, consider yourself fairly warned.

* Hugs

So, my fine friends, sit back on your comfy couches and listen to what went down last year in my cray-cray neck of the woods.

Chapter 1
Shine On, Harvest Moon

Just call me brazen.

It occurs to me that *brazen*—unabashedly bold and without an inkling of shame—is the perfectly appropriate word to describe *moi* right about now. It is, however, the only *perfectly appropriate* part of this evening. Which is perfectly appropriate, in my humble opinion. So get over it.

I lift my chin just enough to stop the stiff orange spikes of glitter-gelled hair from flopping forward onto my forehead. But who can blame me? These spikes are razor sharp—best they stay upright on my head where they belong—and gravity can only do so much to that end.

Okaaaayyyy... sidetracked much?

* Forces rebellious thoughts on business at hand.

Chance César is a brazen B.

I stare 'em down, but only after I pop the collar of the blinding "Orange Crush" tuxedo I'm rockin' and shrug my shoulders in a sort of *what-the-fuck* fashion. Rule of thumb in this queen's life   first things must *always* come first.

Pop, shrug, and *only then* is it kosher to stare.

* Clears throat.

"Eat your ginger-haired heart out, Prince Harry." Based on the buzz of scandalized chatter blowing about in the crisp evening breeze, I'm reasonably certain that *nobody* in the crowd heard me speak. And although several of the girls currently gawking at me may do double backflips over my red-haired counterpart across the pond, Prince Harry of Wales, they don't give a rat's ass about Chance César. In fact, I have a sneaking suspicion that they view my atomic tangerine locks as more reminiscent of Bozo the Clown than of the sexy singer-songwriter Ed Sheeran.

They are, however, completely unaware that this carrot top is going to make Harvest Moon Festival history tonight.

Refusing to succumb to the impulse to duck my head, I take a single shaky step forward on the stage that's been set up on the dusty ground beside the vast (by New England standards) cornfield. The stage doesn't wobble, but my knees sure as shit do. Okay, so I'm a freaking *honest* diva and I tell it like it is. And I'm what you might call a wreck.

Nonetheless, this brazen B takes a deep breath, blows it out in a single gush, and starts to strut. I mean, this boy's werkin' it.

Smi-zeee!! Yeah, my smile is painted on, just like my trousers.

Chance, you are by far the edgiest Miss Harvest Moon this ramshackle town has ever had the good fortune to gaze upon.

I am a major fan of positive self-talk.

Using the feigned British accent that I've perfected—thanks to long hours of tedious practice in my bathroom—I dish out my next thought aloud. "I wish I'd put in a tad more practice walking in these bloody heels before going public in 'em." And despite one slight stumble—a close call to be sure—the clicking sound my pumps make is crisp and confident. I saunter out onto the catwalk.

#trueconfessions: Faking foreign accents is a hobby of mine. I can yammer it up in improvised French, German, Mexican, Russian, and plenty more accents, but I don't mimic Asian languages, as it seems too close to ridicule. My plan for the rest of the night is to continue vocalizing my abundant thoughts in Standard British, with just a hint of Cockney thrown in for charm. New Hampshire is the "live free or die" state and I'll do what I laaaa-like. Yaaasss!

"Introducing this year's lovely... or, um, *handsome* Miss...ter... Harvest Moon. Let's hear an enthusiastic round of applause for Chance César!" Mrs. Higgins always speaks using a lolling Southern twang, although I'm sure she's lived her entire life right here in less-than-gentile, way-too-many-dirt-roads, Fiske, New Hampshire. Like, can you say "backwoods Fiske" without it sounding too much like "backwards Fiske"? But, overall, I'm pleased—it seems I'm not the only one with an affinity for a colorful accent.

The applause is—to be real—disappointingly, but not surprisingly, scattered.

"Woot!" A solitary hoot splits the night—it's quite impossible to miss—and I recognize an undeniably shrill and nasal quality in the sound. I know without a doubt that the hooter is my best (only) friend, Emily Benson. In my not so humble opinion, Emily's hooting *for my benefit* sounds as liberating as Lady Gaga bellowing "Born This Way" live on the Grammy Awards after emerging from a large egg.

My Emily is everything!! Not to be dramatic.

In any case, that single, supportive hoot is followed by *mucho* expected heckling.

"Chances are, Chance César is gonna *moon* the crowd!" That's a girl's voice, for sure. I do *not* have a lot of female fans here in Fiske.

"Come on, Miss Harvest Moon, bend over and flash us your *full moon!*" A dude mocks me next. I'm proud to say that I'm an equal opportunity victim of harassment.

I don't blink once in the face of the jeering. This type of inconvenience is par for the course in my life, and thus, I consider it a challenge. I simply place one fine pointy-toed pump in front of the other, my eyes focused on the mountain in the distance. I'm especially proud that, amidst the chaos, I remember to offer the crowd my best beauty queen wave.

#beautypageantrealness

"Thank you for being here today," I speak in my most Princess Diaries-esque tone.

"*Werk it*, girlfriend—*werk hard!*" Yes, it's Emily again. She's got my back.

"Aw, shit… we must be havin' a *lunar eclipse* or somethin'." It's another pubescent male voice, and a deep one, at that. "There ain't no moon to be seen 'round these parts!" The heckler is a douche I know too well from school, Edwin Darling—whom I less than fondly, and very privately, refer to as "Eddie the Appalling." I watch as he glances up briefly at the full moon in the dark night sky and shrugs.

The lunar eclipse one-liner is actually pretty funny—I toss out ten points for creativity in Edwin's general direction by allowing a small smile—but still I never remove my eyes from the single treeless spot on Mount Vernier.

* Takes a mental detour

I wonder why this one spot is bare-assed of all trees.

That's when the music starts and I'm more than glad for the downbeat. It's much easier to sashay to the sound of a jazzy snare drum than to the unpleasant clamor of heckling. Not that my backside won't wiggle righteously to any sound at all. Because, rest assured, it will.

"Shine On, Harvest Moon." Whoever is in charge of the sound system plays the Liza Minnelli version, which may be the silver lining to this farce. For as long as I can remember, it's been the traditional tune for Miss Harvest Moon's victorious stroll up and down the creaky runway. I will say that tonight is a first for the Liza rendition, and I'm curious as to whether it is coincidental, as she is a female gay icon for the ages.

But who really cares? *Ring them sparkly silver bells for Liza M!!!*

On a side note, I wonder: Is it a good thing or a bad thing that Liza Minnelli's voice always brings out the dramatic streak in me?

Okay, okaaaayyyy... so maybe it doesn't take more than a gentle nudge to get me going in a theatrical direction—but, hey, drama ain't a crime. Momentarily, my mind is pulled to the back of my bedroom closet (how ironic), where my flapper get-up hangs.

Should I have worn that instead?

But it's a muted peach, not a vivid orange, as seems fitting for a pumpkin festival. And then there's the whole "not a single soul, with the exceptions of my parents and Emily, has yet been privileged with the honor of viewing Chance César in full female garb" thing that held me back from rockin' that vintage coral dress with its spectacular tiers of flesh-colored fringe. But tonight is the Beans and Green Farm's Annual Harvest Moon Festival, and for northern New Hampshire, this is a big deal—the whole town shows up for cheesy shit like this.

In light of that recognition, I decide that pumpkin orange attire is mandatorbs. I mean, I went so far as to dye my hair for tonight's festivities; the least I can do is choose garments that enhance the Halloween-like atmosphere.

At the end of the catwalk, I indulge the audience by providing them with their deepest desire: I stand there, still as a statue—for ten seconds, give or take—so they can drink in the sight of me, from spiky glittering head to pointy patent leather toes. I allow them this opportunity for viewing pleasure because *I* know that whether they admire me for having the balls to strut around ultraconservative Fiske wearing a scandalously snug-in-all-the-wrong (right)-places orange tuxedo and four-inch black pumps, which I will admit is a public first for me, or they wish the shining harvest moon would fall on my house and crush me while I sleep, what they all *really* want most is a good long moment to study me.

To twerk or not to twerk, that is the question.

When the spectators finally start to squirm, I throw out a few of my best vogue fem moves to the tune of some subtle arm, wrist, and hand action, followed by several full-body poses, avoiding the death drop move as I haven't yet mastered it in pumps.

And when it's time to once again get this show on the road, I pivot on my toes and strut briskly—picture it, America's Next Top Model style—back to the stage where my boss, the owner of Beans and Greens Farm, stands nervously holding my crown.

Mrs. Higgins is a tall glass of water, in the manner of a big-boned Iowa farm girl, but she's accustomed to crowning petite high school junior girls, not nearly grown senior boys in four-inch heels. I crouch politely, and I dare say delicately, beside her and she carefully nestles the crystal-studded crown in my spiky mop of neon orange hair.

"Be careful, Mrs. H," I warn her beneath my breath. "Those spikes might look harmless, but they're sharp enough to slice off your little finger."

She offers me half of a crooked smile, for which I give her credit. I, Mrs. Higgins' very own "boy with the bad attitude on cash register three", have broken about every rule Beans and Greens has established for its hordes of Fiske High School summer workers, right down to the "no jewelry at work" clause. But a couple of points go to the lady cuz she manages to force out a grimace that *could* be mistaken for a smile… if your standard for smiles is on the low side.

Besides, I'm not about to remove my nose ring. It in no way impedes my ability to count, ring up, and bag cucumbers.

* Spins on a single heel to face the crowd.

"You don't happen to have any… *very brief…* words of wisdom for our audience, do you, Chance?" Mrs. Higgins asks, speaking into an oversized microphone. But despite the laidback accent, I can tell she's wary. Like a rat in a corner.

"Yes, as a matter of fact, I do." My clipped British accent momentarily stuns the woman, and I take that opportunity to snatch the microphone from her less-than-dainty hand. Realizing that it is now in my possession, Mrs. Higgins shudders. "I just want to thank you all, my *beloved* co-workers at Beans and Greens Farm, for voting me in as this year's Miss Harvest Moon." I wipe imaginary tears from my eyes with my wrist, sniff for added effect, and, of course, I employ a most gracious, high-pitched tone of voice. "I am just *so honored* to represent you all here tonight." I sound like Eliza Doolittle in the stage play *My Fair Lady*.

The crowd is silent. Maybe it's a stunned silence. *I sincerely hope so.*

* Pouty lips follow dainty sniffling. *Sniff, sniff.*

Mrs. Higgins makes a sudden grab for the microphone but I'm more ag-ile. I only have to twist my shoulders ever so slightly to the left to block her move.

Then I lower my voice so it's all man—momentarily losing the delightful British inflection—and I pose my question to the crowd. "So you thought voting for me as Miss Harvest Moon, here, would humiliate me—dull my shine or rain on my parade, perhaps?" I wag my well-manicured finger at the crowd. "Well, in your face, my sorry backwoods homies, cuz I'm *here* and I'm *queer* and I'm shining on—just like that big ol' harvest moon!" Without hesitation, I lean down just enough to grab Mrs. Higgins around the waist, and then I lift her off her feet and swing that lady around, probs 'til she's seeing more stars than the ones in the dark Harvest Moon sky.

I'd bet my ahhh-mazing ass that no other Miss Harvest Moon has ever given Mrs. Higgins a joyride like that!

Chapter 2
Late Night Jazz

After my coronation, I change back into my usual attire, a Juilliard School logo hoodie sweatshirt—a fine choice, even if Emmy is completely obsessed by the college—and skinny jeans (natch) rolled up to the ankles to show off my bright yellow Converse Chuck Taylor All Stars. And then there are the eye-catching additions of the *Miss Harvest Moon* sash across my torso and, of course, the sparkling tiara, giving me life! Woot!

Glancing around in search of Emily and coming up empty, I do the pop (my hoodie, in this case), shrug, and stare move, and then head to the fence by the cornfield for the carved pumpkin competition. I can practically feel the wad of bills I'm going to win stuffed into the back pocket of my skinny jeans, right beside all of the unruly thoughts I keep hidden there. A crowded place, my back pocket is.

"Channy—found you!" Emily jumps up and grabs me by my waist and then sort of swings around like she's a pole dancer and I'm her stripper pole. She's more of a burden than she realizes, but I freaking adore every inch and pound of her.

"Werk it, bitch," I say. She does. Emily swings around my midsection, her lips forming these seductive shapes I'm less than comfortable with, and then she hockey stops abruptly on my left side. "Nobody's gonna be able to beat my Mona Lisa pumpkin, Emily. *Nobody*." I'm still using a British accent, but Emily either doesn't notice or is immune to my antics, and doesn't give a crap.

She reaches up and hangs from my neck a moment longer, her fingertips now digging painfully into my skin. Then she laughs really loud as she drops to the ground, her auburn French braids bouncing around on her shoulders. Side note: delete "laughs" and replace with "guffaws" in the interest of accuracy.

"By the end of tonight I'm gonna be Miss Harvest Moon *and* The Beans and Greens Pumpkin Carving King!"

"Talk about gender fluidity."

That comment momentarily shuts me up for reasons I'd prefer not to go into, but for the sake of this story, I will. I'm simply not one for fancy labels… or any labels at all, for that matter. I'm simply satisfied with being spectacular. Now, it *is* possible that if I could *find* a label to accurately define me, I'd embrace it. I have so far been unsuccessful in that quest. So I'm sticking with this philosophy: There's no immediate need to define the boundaries of Chance César's fabulousness.

Subject closed.

"That's because Mona Lisa the pumpkin is the bee's knees, truly."

"Totes," I mumble, aware that Emmy (for the purposes of this story, Emily, Em, Emmy are all interchangeable) is oblivious that she stuck her foot in it, and deeply, with the gender remark. And beyond that, I'm not exactly sure whether she thinks people still say things like "the bee's knees", or if she is *trying* to be retro-original. With Emily, sometimes it's hard to know.

Emily and I are an uncool-kid force to be reckoned with. I certainly do detest the days when Emily's absent from school, because on those occasions I'm reminded of the meaning of the term "solitary confinement".

"You rocked those pumps on the runway, Channy. 'Cept for the first time you stopped and posed."

"I nearly fell off the catwalk right then."

She nods and casts a matter-of-fact glance my way. I instinctively know this is not big news to her. Emily had been present for my single high-heel-strutting practice session in the upstairs hallway off my bedroom. "Wouldn't a flying leap from the catwalk have surprised the bejesus out of Edwin fucker-nelly Darling?"

"Fucker-nelly?"

"New word."

"You just made it up?"

"Of course." She looks at me with an expression that says, "Duh!" more clearly than words can. She then lifts her already turned-up nose into the air with clear exasperation at my apparent dimwittedness.

While I changed my clothes, Mrs. Higgins and company had placed each pumpkin entry on the top of a fence post and had lit the candles inside them. The exhibition of pumpkins stretches out along the fence for the entire length of the cornfield. Parents and kids and old folks and tons of teenagers and even the local newspaper, The Fiske Daily Democrat (hardly— this town defines Republican), mill around, checking out the long rows of carved pumpkins.

I catch a little girl eyeing my crown with envy and I shoot her a look that says, "Back off, little girl! This crown is mine! Go win your own damned beauty pageant." I'm kind of good at knowing what people, from little girls to old men, are thinking. In fact, I have a sixth sense that tells me a high percentage of the lurking teenagers' fingers are itching to do some pumpkin smashing.

"There are plenty of decent carvings here," I say blandly. Emmy already knows where I'm going with this, I'm sure. She's well aware of my competitive streak, which at times enhances (conflicts with) my dramatic streak.

"Well, sure. There are the standard goofy and scary faces, of course, and people have gotten quite creative with the concept of teeth."

"That could be the understatement of the Harvest Moon Festival." My accent slips. I see pumpkins with fangs and long rows of pearly whites. Half a dozen have multiple rows of teeth and gaping holes where teeth should be. Dr. Pidgeon, the local orthodontist, would have a field day with these unfortunate fellows.

Emmy and I move so that we're standing in front of one of those long thin pumpkins balancing precariously on a post. It's been turned onto its side and carved into a pirate ship. Featured elements are sails made out of leaves and tiny acorn pirates. Not too shabby at all.

"Hmmm…." She lingers before it, her eyes narrowing. Pricks of anxiety rise up my spine as I wait for her judgment.

"This one is damned good." All traces of my intriguing Brit/Cockney inflection are now lost.

"Don't wig out—Mona Lisa is still better."

It's uncanny how well this girl knows me, I think, and then, because I know *her* impulsive brain equally well, *and* because she crouches slightly into a position resembling a cat preparing to pounce, I brace myself for the likely event of being publicly, yet playfully, body-slammed. I'm on the tall and skinny side—but don't get me wrong, I can take it if Emily pounces, as long as I'm ready.

"Well, of course Mona is the superior pumpkin," I reply, my fake English accent suddenly back in working order. "I'd challenge an art critic to find a bloody flaw in her."

Instead of jumping on me Emily grabs my hand and pulls me toward the next fence post, and we silently gawk at the pumpkin on display. "Gross… I mean, that one's fucker-nelly disgusting."

"Yeah… totes sick." Everybody knows that "sick" is a compliment these days, so I'm actually *disagreeing* with my BFF. I hesitate a second, again trying to figure out what part of speech Emily's newly created word "fucker-nelly" is. "I think this pumpkin's kind of funny, hun. Like in-your-face-ralphing-realness."

Nobody at school can say that Chance César is lacking in a sense of humor, even if I *am* the butt of an unhealthily high percentage of the jokes there. So I'm all about this sick pumpkin that has been fashioned to look like it's barfing out its own seeds. We move down the line to check out the next pumpkin.

Emily takes one look at it, rubs her rounded belly, and declares, "I'm hungry."

A pumpkin with a pi sign carved into the front. "Pumpkin pi... that's clever."

But is it clever enough to rival Mona Lisa? I doubt it. *Hehehe.*

Holding hands, we saunter along the fence that separates the field from the road. We see several Bob Marleys in pumpkin form, a pumpkin Red Sox player, and a round, orange likeness of Oprah Winfrey. And on the ground beside the fence, a pumpkin snowman. My confidence grows.

And then we both see it at the same time. I squeeze Emmy's hand so hard she whimpers. "Go ahead and say what we're both thinking." I sound bitchy, but hey, bitchy ain't a crime.

"It's good." She looks up at me, her eyes wide. "As in, fucker-nelly good."

I don't know if Emily's chin has dropped as far as mine, because once I begin to stare at the glorious bright orange work of art before me, my eyes are simply stuck there. And although I have suddenly gained the insight that *fucker-nelly* is most commonly used as an adverb, my soul is suffused with a profound sense of loss. *Poof*—just like that, the imaginary wad of bills disappears from my back pocket.

Until tonight I was the undisputed top pumpkin carver in these parts, and the loss of that status smarts. But even worse, the twisted satisfaction of simultaneously being both the king *and* the queen of this hokey event is gone, gone, gone.

Together, we take a step forward to examine the amazing, illuminated carousel. Whoever carved it found a perfectly round pumpkin with which to work. The artist—and I don't say that lightly because true artists are few and far between—cut graceful horses with delicate poles around its entire circumference, and then made a canopy on top that is so ornate and detailed I pinch my arm because I think maybe I'm dreaming. It's completely hollow. I can see through it to the dopey face of the little boy staring in awe on its other side, and I wonder why it doesn't collapse in on itself. Next, I wonder if I blow with force on the master-fucking-piece, whether maybe I can roll it over. And yes, I know, it's a freaking pumpkin—but it's in a delicate and airy, even magical, form. More than Cinderella's tricked out midnight ride. My guess is it wouldn't look so breathtaking resting on its side.

Cue the evil laughter. *Mwah ha ha!*

Maybe for just a split second I wish the damned thing would collapse—like my nose did beneath Eddie the Appalling's fist last fall—but I quickly take that wish back because I'm all for fair play. I am, really.

Neither Emily nor I are in possession of the appropriate words for this occasion, and speechlessness occurs about once in a blue moon for us. We just stand there and gawk. I even drool slightly; the carousel carving is *that* freaking fabulous. I just can't help myself. I only wipe my chin when another pumpkin-gawker joins us. I refrain from glancing in his direction, though. Aloof is how I always play it.

"I liked your tuxedo… y' know, up there on the runway. You looked great."

Don't look at him, Chance.

Instead of turning to stare, I perform a vocal analysis: it's a low, smooth, maybe somewhat husky, male voice. And it's young. The voice belongs to a teenager.

Moments like this call for what I refer to as *strategic reaction*.

Should I be bitchy? *" 'Great?' You think I went to all that trouble to look 'great?' Try 'drop-dead gorgeous', mister, and maybe I'll toss you a 'merci, monsieur'."* But speaking French will clash with my English accent, so that response is out.

Maybe I should go with gracious. *"Oh, thank you, dear. I am just so over-whelmingly proud to be honored with the title of Miss Harvest Moon."*

My response usually depends on the asker's intention. Is he being cruel or kind? In my experience, cruel usually wins the contest hands down. But this time I'm not so sure.

Thankfully, Emily relieves me of my need to respond. "Chance knocked everybody dead up there. Have you ever seen a tuxedo so tubular?"

Tubular? Oh, Emmy….

Again, that gentle, lyrical voice. "Um… no. I don't think I ever have."

Call me a sucker, but the guy sounds sweet and genuine—at least enough to merit a few measly points. I bestow upon him a brief five-point sideways glance. No, I don't actually move my head in his direction, but I do allow for the shifting of my eyeballs.

"Holy fucker-nelly!" I use Emily's new word totally incorrectly—I've already established that fucker-nelly is *not* a noun. But I can't be blamed for grammatical blunders, especially not when they're spoken with a perfect English flair. That is, however, like totes beside the point—the guy with the sweet voice is smoking hot. And just like that, Chance César is smitten.

I'm not sure, however, that smitten is a positive state for me seeing as I again find myself abnormally tongue-tied, not to mention a tad bit warm beneath my hoodie.

"I'm Jasper. Jasper Donahue. And, like I said, I thought your tuxedo was cool." He swallows rather obviously and reaches out to shake my hand. We shake and I can't miss the rough hands and strong grip. "And your speech was good, too."

My speech was "good?" It was designed to piss people off.

"I voted for ya. For Miss Harvest Moon, y' know?"

Now *this* is getting interesting. "Tell me, *why* did you vote for me, Jazz?" He smiles when I call him that.

Another hobby of mine is making up nicknames for people. I like to morph their real names into more fitting versions. And Jasper's voice—low and smooth and smoky and melodic—Jazz to me now and forever.

Yes, I know. Dramatic as all get-out. But so what?

Emmy and I stare at Jazz with the same level of intense scrutiny that we'd applied to the work-of-art pumpkin carousel. "All of the workers here just voted for Channy to make fun of him! You're nothing but an asshole." Maybe Emily's scrutiny would better be labeled as contempt.

My dear best friend's worst habit is that she allows herself to get riled up far too easily. And then she gets verbally offensive, followed closely by physically abusive—all at the drop of a hat. I notice Emmy winding up to throw a punch, and I move strategically between Jazz and her. "Em, sweetie, go and get your Channy a cup of hot cider, would you?"

She appears pissed off to the max to have been interrupted. It crosses my mind that she may actually slug *me*. "I'm not leaving you here alone with this asshole." Her hands shakily find her hips but I can tell the restraint takes great effort.

I will admit that Jazz appears completely confounded at this point. I will also admit that confused looks utterly adorbs on the guy. "I'm fine, Emmy. Except that I'm thirsty." I send her my best "meaningful" look, which translates to, "take a hike, hunny—I can handle this one all by my lonely."

After a final glare—a warning one at Jazz this time—my BFF takes off in the direction of the cider stand.

"So you voted for Chance César to be Miss Harvest Moon?" I ask sweetly. And I'm talking sugar-frosted-honey-coated-candy sweet. With caramel drizzled on it.

Jazz looks at the ground like he's ashamed. I don't miss the opportunity to size him up. Jazz Donohue is just slightly shorter than me, but makes up for it with muscles. Yeah, he's ripped. At least, from what I can see beneath his T-shirt and jeans, he's ripped enough to satisfy *my* needs. Brown hair, cut short, dark eyes, with lashes I'd kill for, and a guileless friendly face. Possibly something less than a rocket scientist judging by his simple expression, but I have no desire to explore space with the dude.

"Your name was on the ballot," Jazz says, his voice uncertain and slightly defensive. "Your name was on the ballot and so I voted for you." He hesitates for a moment, and then looks up at me. "You're smarter and funnier…

16

and prettier, too," he says that last part softly. "And I knew you'd be a way better Miss Harvest Moon than Stella Gordon or Jamie-Lynne Slater." I wish it wasn't so dark. I could see if he's blushing, as I suspect he may be.

I think, *No shit Sherlock*. I say, "But we don't know each other, Jazz."

He looks back down at his work boots. "I know *you*… you just haven't noticed me yet."

Not many people are capable of pulling the rug out from beneath my feet. I mean, I live ready to bite back. But rugged Jazz, in his dirty white T-shirt and well-worn jeans, a navy blue and green plaid flannel tied low on his waist, has knocked me flat.

"You work here too?" I try to sound like it makes no difference to me but my effort is an epic fail.

Jazz nods and turns away slightly, like he's planning to cut and run. "There are days I plant and pick, but mostly, I do odd jobs. Y' know, I fix things and stuff."

"I, uh… I think I remember seeing you building the cat walk." Come to think of it, I actually do.

"*And* I go to school with you at Fiske High. Only thing is, I'm in the vocational program, so for the most part we're never in the same wing of the building."

Well, you could have easily knocked me over with a brilliantly colored male peacock feather. I have absolutely no recollection of Jazzy-boy here from school, and I'm fairly observant. It's silent for a few seconds, and curiously, I scramble for something to say to keep him beside me. "This carousel pumpkin," nodding at the elegant pumpkin in front of us, I admit the truth before thinking it through, "… it might just be the best one here."

That's when Jazz smiles broadly and I decide his smile is the most honest and straightforward smile I've ever seen. "*I* carved this pumpkin, Chance. I made it for my little sister."

I think I gasp, as I hadn't expected burly Jazzy to be the Michelangelo of pumpkin carving. "Well, your sister is a very lucky girl." I smile at him, confident in the knowledge that he's the guy who is going to take the title of Beans and Greens Pumpkin Carving King away from me.

He grins again and I fight the urge to pinch his adorbs cheek. I find it a difficult urge to battle.

I have lost nothing. Tonight is a win-win for Chance César. Cuz I met Jazz.

"I gotta head. My little sister's here somewhere and it's time to bring her home—she's got Sunday school in the morning. But 'fore I go, I gotta ask you one thing."

He's going to ask me for a date, I can feel it in my bones. If he does, it'll be a first for me. My throat tightens in excited apprehension cuz I think it's possible that this guy is gonna be mine.

"You got the coolest way of talkin', Chance. You from England, big guy?"

Chapter 3
Lost: One Rat's Ass, $10,000 Reward if Found and Returned In Good Condition to Rightful Owner

My parents are what you might call "rather apathetic" with regard to their sentiments toward the one who will, in theory, carry on the César name. Or at least that's how I see it. Fair warning—I'm a person who likes to call spades exactly what they are. And even if I *so badly* wish the spade was a club, I still call the frigging thing a spade. So yeah, when I was young, I used to pretend like Mom and Dad gave a crap, but you can only pretend for so damned long. Now that I'm seventeen, any and all remnants of the "I love you, you love me—we're a happy family" charade are ancient history.

Nope. They don't give a rat's ass about their only child, Chance.

Now don't get me wrong—Mom and Dad possess no wish for lousy shit to fly my way. They just aren't into the whole parenting thing, and I figure that's their right.

But on the brighter side, they don't give a rat's ass that I'm gay. Nope, there's no horrific, scarring homophobia going on in the César family home. And get this: my big "coming out of the closet" last year consisted of three lines of dialogue between my parents and moi:

Me: Mom, Dad... I'm gay... and I just thought you guys might want to know.
Dad (yawning): That's nice, Chance.
Mom: Yeah, that's great. Oh, by the way, it's get-your-own-dinner-night... again.

Nope, nothing emotionally scarring there.

Good thing I'm the kind of guy who chooses to focus on the positive. I can walk around the house in full female stripper garb, and nobody bats an eyelash. If I conjure up any reaction at all, it might be that my mother asks me where I bought my sexy stretch-lace naughty knickers, as she's been looking for ones in that color. And speaking of color choices, neither Mom nor Dad said a single word when I showed up with my hair dyed the flamboyant shade of a Cheez Doodle. Not only do I have complete freedom with how I express my personal style, but when I go all drama-queen mode on their asses, my parents just look at each other and shrug. In fact, I try—and I try fucker-nelly hard—but I just can't shock these people.

I can barely get them to notice me.

They're always too busy *noticing* other things—their business mostly. They own a hippy-dippy gift shop in the tourist town of Charisse, down by the lake. It takes up ninety-nine percent of their time and attention. I will say, if you happen to be remotely into the Grateful Dead, you really shouldn't miss a visit to *The Sugar Magnolia Gift Shop* on Main Street in Charisse. (Its financial success funds my escapades.)

The bright side... the bright side... I must insist you look on the bright side, you brazen B.

Here's another sparkling aspect of the bright side with regard to Mom and Dad's persistent indifference towards moi—it's not a slight problem for me to have my female best friend sleep over almost every weekend. Nobody here gives a bleep who I sleep with... or if I sleep at all. And Emmy's parents feel bad for me and they know that we're "just friends", plus with the added protection of knowing I'm gay, they let her sleep over once a week. So, on the nights she comes over, it's kind of like I have a family, if not a very small one. Yeah, each week on Friday or Saturday night I'm "the family guy", and that's better than nothing.

I'm really fine with the situation as it stands. Mom, Dad, and I coexist quite comfortably. And I ain't joshin'.

I wouldn't do that. Really....

***

"I'm stuffed." Emily flops back on my big bed and then kicks the empty pizza box to the floor with a stuffed-dachshund-slippered foot. She runs her fingers absently through her long reddish-brown hair that she recently released from the confines of the French braids she wears daily, like a hair-uniform. Her loose hair now falls past her shoulders, glorious in a warped and twisted way I entirely can relate to.

I pull my silky light blue robe around me more snugly and then retie the waist just because I feel like it.

#trueconfession: I simply adore the feeling of this robe's silky smoothness on my skin; it actually gives me goose bumps. Often I can't wait to come home from school and art club or work, just so I can put on my robe and my silky pajama pants and curl up on my soft bed. Only then can I stop thinking so much for a while.

Emmy is one of three people in the world who has seen this *different* side of moi. FYI: I *choose* to think of it as my soft side rather than my feminine side—I've never been all about sorting out that complicated part of myself. My motto has long been, "Gender Labels Suck Donkey Balls", but tonight isn't one of those space-out-and-feel-the-silk nights, cuz Emmy's here. And also because meeting Jazz has reawakened my impulse to wonder what the bleep I am. In the gender department, that is.

Not to fear—there will be more on that later. I promise.

Before I plant myself beside Emily on my queen-sized bed that I recently draped in a bolt of lime green chiffon, I bend and pick up the pizza box from the floor and stick it on my desk. I scoop up our soda bottles from the night table and toss them into the recycling bin, and then I finally grab my laptop. "I don't live in a barn, Emmy."

She snorts at me in the manner of a round pink farm animal.

I'm pleased that my British accent is still going strong. I don't even have to think at this point—it just pops out of my mouth as if I was born in Liverpool. On my way to the bed I say, "I have this idea...."

"Before you tell me, Channy, brush that gel out of your hair. If you stab me in my sleep with one of those spikes, I'll bleed out."

What she said has merit, so I grab my hairbrush and then plunk down on the bed, causing her to bounce on the mattress. As I brush my jagged orange hair, I start to talk. "What did you think of Jasper Donahue, Emmy?"

"This year's Beans and Greens Pumpkin Carving King?"

"The one and only."

"His pumpkin was amazeballs." She kicks off her puppy slippers. "But he was one of the kids who voted for you to be Miss Harvest Moon."

"I think he voted for me because he...."

"Yeah?"

"He told me he thought I'd make the best Miss Harvest Moon."

"Well, he was right. Do you know him from school?"

I shake my half-spiky head.

"I do. We... uh... we were in a required health class together last year." She's struggling to tell me something.

"Spill it, BFF. Let's keep it real, for the love of Neil Patrick Harris."

She sighs. Loudly. "Look, I'm not one to criticize, but... Jasper Donahue is not exactly the sharpest knife in the drawer."

"You mean tool in the shed?"

"No. I mean knife in the drawer. You're like a rocket scientist compared to him."

I don't care... He liked my tuxedo. He thinks I'm smart and funny... and pretty.

"So what's your point?" I ask—my accent may have dried up, but my inner bitch is now an outer bitch.

"That is my point. You could run circles around that kid. He's not up to your… like, your level of 'clued in'." She makes those air quotes, which never fails to piss me off. Such a cool-kid gesture.

"Haven't you ever heard the expression 'still waters run deep'? And aren't you Miss High-and-Mighty?"

"I'm just sayin'."

"I don't think I want to discuss this any further with you." I pull off my robe.

"I sure messed the hell outta what I was trying to…." In a second, Emily is scooting to my side of the bed. "So sorry, Channy. I just thought… oh, never mind. Tell me about your big idea. It involves Jasper, right?"

I lean toward the night table and turn the light off. Emily's practically on top of me at this point, so close I can feel her breath on my bare shoulder. "It's really more of a plan." I use my coy voice because I know it drives her crazy and I owe her one. "Cuz maybe I'm into the boy."

I can't explain how I feel any better than that. I don't have a clue if Jazz is gay or straight, and I don't really know if I want him to see me as a chick or a dude, or a combination of both. I just know I like what I see when I look at Jazz Donahue.

Luckily Emmy asks no questions in regard to my gender quandary. She is too distracted by my plan. "You come up with the best ideas." Her breathing slows, and then speeds up to an abnormal rate, which is not at all surprising to me. I've seen Emily display this peculiar pattern of breathing before. "Please don't keep me in suspense."

"Well, say it, then." We have a standard line of apology that we deliver to each other when one of us misbehaves. It makes our apologies official.

Another loud sigh. "I have been a very naughty girl and I'm sorry, so spank me… *okay?* I shouldn't have dissed Jasper. Happy now? Just tell me about this plan!"

"Okay, so here's the deal…." Our heads drift together like they have so many times before. And I admit to myself that it's a good thing I brushed the spikes out of my hair, or I would have probs poked one of Emmy's eyes out.

#secretplanrealness Uh-huh.

Chapter 4
The Fault of My Bears

Emmy is dead on. When I see him, I nearly choke on the gummy bear I'm chewing. Just like she said, there he is, sitting at a table in the back of the caf by the floor-to-ceiling windows. As luck would have it, Jasper Donahue has lunch Block B, which is smack-dab in the middle of my free period. With Tessa McGill across from him and Kyle Marone beside him, two kids I remember from middle school but haven't given so much as a thought since they went to the voc' and I went college prep, he shovels school mac and cheese into his mouth. And I think he likes it seeing as he shuts his eyes for a split second each time he takes a bite. Which is kinda hot.

Okaaayyy, so maybe it totes slays me. (Not. A. Crime.)

I experience a surge of confidence and tell myself I can pull off the early stages of The Plan. I strutted down a freaking catwalk, for crying out loud—in a neon orange tux and patent leather pumps. This is a cakewalk by comparison.

Chance and Emmy's Can Not/Will Not Fail Plan
A. The approach

"OMG! If it isn't The Harvest Moon Pumpkin Carving King, himself? So you weren't pulling a fast one on me—you actually *do* go to Fiske High." I have no idea if he's gonna buy that I just *so happened* to require a sip of water from the fountain on the *back wall* of the cafeteria, but I don't let that minor detail deter me. I take a quick drink from the fountain and then slide onto the bench beside him. I don't get too close because there's no shortage of guys, in my experience, who freak out when the school's lone gay kid moves into their personal space.

When he hears my voice, Jazz drops his spoon. As it clangs on his lunch tray, I have to smile. People only drop their silverware when they give a rat's ass. At least I'm gonna interpret the spoon-drop that way.

"Chance? Hey, dude... I didn't know you had lunch this block."

Um... yeah. I choose to ignore that minor detail. I *do* have a free period, but I'm supposed to be using it constructively. Like, say, studying in the library, filling out college apps in guidance, reviewing chorus music in practice room C—*not* picking up boys in the cafeteria. My *real* lunch block is D, an hour from now. "So, anyway, Jazz...."

His friends look at each other, confused by my presence at their lunch table, as well as by my use of the pet name that suits Jasper Donahue so totes perfectly. And I instinctively know it's time to put The Plan into action. The other night, Emmy and I came to the mutual conclusion that I should start small, and number one on the list is essentially ground zero.

So I break into a brilliant smile. No, *brilliant* is far too weak a word, not doing justice to my impeccably straight white teeth—I wore braces on my stubbornly crooked teeth for four-and-a-half goddamn years to get them into line—and to my slim, well-Cherry-Chapsticked lips. I scour my mind for the correct adjective. *Amazeballs* doesn't work. It simply doesn't conjure up an image of the witty intelligence coupled with the spicy hotness that my smile possesses. *Awesomesauce…* no, not so much. *Smexy*? Yes, *smexy* will do nicely.

B. Putting The Plan into action

My lips curve into a super smexy smile….

It's obvious that The Target has absolutely no idea why I'm smiling at him like he just broke the birthday piñata. He turns around to check behind him, as if maybe the reason for my cheerful grin is there. When he turns back to face me, I force myself to maintain steady eye contact; my lips are starting to quiver as if *they* are the jittery brains behind this whole operation but I refuse to release them from their stiffly jubilant pose.

My mind drifts back to the sleepover when Emmy and I did the research. The list we found in the Today's Lady online article clearly stated: Number One—Smile well and often. And dammit, I intend to do this thing right, so I scour my brain to recall the article's finer points in regard to item number one. Cuz everybody knows that the genius (devil) is in the details. Now, hadn't the article mentioned a highly effective measure that called for tucking my hair behind one ear, tilting my head ever so slightly, and breaking into a slowly growing smile? And if I'm not dreaming, it said a blush would serve me well at this point, too. Reportedly, the visual combo package—tuck, tilt, smile, and blush—is irresistible to all men everywhere. I set "TTSB" into motion.

Jazz smiles back. It is the same warm, open, and easy smile that he bestowed upon me at the Harvest Moon Pumpkin Festival as we stood studying his prize-winning carving. "Glad you stopped by to say hi," he says with what might have been a wink, but is probs just a speck of dust and wishful thinking on my part.

For further motivation, as suggested by the online article, I fill my mind with images of "the good things in life"—my silky robe and a supersize tube of glitter hair gel and multiple bottles of Rustic Rosemary nail polish. With these images in mind, my smile can't help but grow wider. "Why thank you,

Jazz. I'm so happy I noticed you on my way to the… to the water fountain."

Jasper Donahue's gaze sinks from my eyes down to my smiling lips, and stays there. For that, I mentally pat myself on the back. This boy's an easy Target. The Plan is already working, and I'm only on number one. He can't keep his eyes off my luscious smiling lips. I feel almost guilty that I got this awesomesauce online advice for free.

"Were you eating gummy bears today?"

Well, that's an odd question. And how does he know? Does Jazz possess a bloodhound's nose for penny candy?

"Why, yes, hun. I indulged in a handful on my way here from the library." I nervously tuck the hair behind my other ear, which isn't part of "TTSB" that strictly instructs, tuck hair behind one ear, not both. "But how did you know?"

Jazz reaches forward with a pointed finger and dislodges something from my right front tooth. He actually has to scrape a bit with his fingernail. "You had a green gummy bear head stuck to your tooth."

My smile pulls that death drop dance move I've recently mastered in my bedroom. Sha-blam! With now tightly closed lips, I nod at The Target and stand up, blushing profusely as I make tracks back to the library.

Chapter 5
A Pie-stroll

"So, what you're telling me, Channy, is that it was a total pie-stroll?"

A huge part of me doesn't want to ask, but the question still spills out of my mouth. "Is *pie-stroll* a new word?"

"Of course," Emily replies, smug as all the kids who'd watched calmly as Eddie the Appalling fed me his fist on a silver-frigging-platter last fall after the final home football game.

"And?"

Yawning, she refuses to acknowledge my inquiry.

Nope. The word-devising diva who is Emily Benson isn't gonna be satisfied until I spell out the question in its entirety. "And what, dare I ask, is the meaning of 'pie-stroll', my dear Miz Merriam-Webster of Improvised Language?"

At that, she breaks into a wide smile. I *so* adore her Emma Stone freckles that set off her Liv Tyler overbite. Her imperfectness is perfection. "You know what a cakewalk is?"

I nod.

"Well, a pie-stroll is even easier than that."

"Fair enough, hunny." I lean forward to take my cup of Cinnamon Swirlee Pumpkin Mousse Extravaganza frozen yogurt from the server, and since he's cute and I don't think he's on any contact sports teams at Fiske High School (contact sports teams spell D.A.N.G.E.R. to a large majority of gay kids), I give him a tiny three-point smile, reminiscent of my Mona Lisa pumpkin. He smiles back at me, and then turns around to scoop Emily's yogurt. The name of her flavor, Mucho Chocolata, is not nearly as flamboyant as mine. And that is as it should be.

When Emily and I have no afterschool activities, we meet at The Brain Freeze Yogurt Shoppe to share decadent, creatively named frozen yogurts and a generous portion of gossip. Today we take our cups of yogurt and sit in the far back corner of the shop so we'll have privacy for our discussion of strategy.

"Well, it wasn't a *complete and total* pie-stroll." I think about the gummy bears I usually have sprinkled liberally on my frozen yogurt, but that I refrained from indulging in today. Just the thought of gummy bears makes my stomach churn. "But, all in all, I think the first part of our plan went as well as we could have hoped for."

"You grinned your ass off?"

"You better believe it."

"Um, *hello!*" Emmy places her cup of yogurt down firmly on the sticky table and makes a big show of licking her spoon. I realize she needs an opportunity to practice all of her newly invented sexy lip motions, but I fervently wish she had another person to practice on. What she doesn't know, however, is that she is wearing this itsy-bitsy, totes adorbs, chocolate moustache, which makes my job of *Official Witness to the Seductive Lip Showcase* far more tolerable. "I want details, César!"

With absolute obedience, I wink and spill. "Well, as we established last weekend, I needed to start with the most basic tactic on the list. And so I went with the logical first choice, number one."

Emmy pulls her MacBook Air out of her backpack. She opens it to the link she's labeled *The List*. On my computer at home it's saved as: *The List for The Plan*, which I realize is an inconsequential detail. So sue me.

I glance at the screen.

Ten Scientifically Proven Ways to Make a Man Fall in Love With You

"The box in front of the first easy step can now be checked," I inform her impassively, as if this is not big news.

1. Smile well and often.

"Tell me about your grand entrance." She continues to shower more physical attention than any spoon has a right to, onto the plastic utensil in her hand.

"Well, girlfriend, I werked it." I take an oversized bite of my Cinnamon Swirlee Pumpkin Mousse Extravaganza frozen yogurt, suffer the ensuing brain freeze like a trooper, and then continue. "I strutted to the water fountain, dove down for a quick sip, and then slid right in beside him at the lunch table, and I *showed him some teeth*."

"Did you make sure the smile reached your eyes?" She touches her computer screen. "It says right here that eye-smiling is—"

"Mandatorbs," I interrupt and nod.

"Did you keep in mind that a smile is your best weapon in the battlefield we refer to as love?"

"I didn't forget that for a second." And I make a sudden decision: If my boo wants details, by God, she's gonna get them. "I rocked the slow smile/hair tuck combo. Managed to blush, too."

"Sha-blam!" I can easily see the pride on her face. "You were simply irresistible."

"That I was." I indulge in another well-earned bite of yogurt.

"And Jasper's reaction?"

I almost feel guilty—getting Jazz's undivided attention had been such a complete pie-stroll. I place the back of one hand flat on the table. Then I point to my palm with my other hand. "I had him eating out of this."

"Well, that is fucker-nelly fantastic! So where do we go from here?" Emmy's freckled skin has turned pink with her eagerness. Not to mention she's actually breathless.

In unison, we peer at the screen. "How about... say, number... two?" I realize that proceeding in numerical order in a matter this complicated is a far-fetched proposition.

We stare at number two critically, as if we need to proofread it for English class.

2. Men fall in love with what they see. Show him the best version of you!

"Okay, Channy. You need to start being hotness personified." Her full lips twist to the side and she bites down on the bottom one with her protruding front teeth. I will admit she looks worried, which irks me.

You be dissin' me? I've got this attractiveness thing in the bag!" I am (almost) unspeakably offended. But I somehow manage to find the perfect words. "I can clean up my act with no problem at all—it'll be a freakin' pie-stroll!"

"You're not exactly Scarlett Johansson." She's throwing shade my way and I don't like it one bit.

"Oh, ye of little faith," I say dismissively. I am much more of a Nicole Kidman type than a Scarlett Johansson type anyway. "I've gotta head."

"Off to the beauty salon?"

"Hardly. Looking fantabulous is child's play for moi." I grab my leopard print backpack and strut toward the door. "I live for this, doll!"

I can hear Emily's noisy guffaw as I make my way out the door.

***

This is a pie-stroll... totes a pie-stroll, I repeat as I stand before my bathroom mirror, my printed list of scientifically proven beauty tips taped to the nearby wall.

* studies show that men find red lips attractive, as they suggest fertility

What the bleep have I gotten myself into?
I speak aloud to the reflection of Chance César who gapes so cluelessly back at me. "Well, that *is* precisely why God invented Cherry Chapstick, dufus!" I inform myself, a heavy dose of sarcasm in my tone. I pop open a fresh tube of lip balm and smear it onto my lips with more than my usual precision.

* flushed cheeks are another desirable sign of youth and fertility—go for a subtle light pink

This one's easy. I pinch my cheeks hard a couple of times, and *ta-daa!* I'm a blushing beauty.

* don't hold back on the eyeliner and mascara—men find outstanding eyes quite sensual

#trueconfession: Applying makeup is an activity I've long wanted to try, but have never had the balls, so to speak, to actually go through with. Over the past year, I've collected a limited number of cosmetics and have stored them in the back of the drawer beneath the bathroom sink. I own several shades of guyliner and have a tube of mascara, ready and waiting for this day to come.
I must admit, I *do* hold back on the mascara, but I go to freakin' town with the black eyeliner. When I'm finished, a ginger Captain Jack Sparrow stares back at me. *Hmmm....*

* spritz on a signature scent—he won't be able to get you out of his mind

Before Mom got home from work today, I borrowed (stole) three types of perfume she keeps in the back of her bathroom closet. In a small Tupperware bowl, I pour liberal quantities of *Utter Damnation, Breath of God, and The Good Earth*, certain that, between these three fragrances, I've covered all of my bases—hell, heaven, and our trusty home planet in between. Then I add a few splashes of my own favorite fragrances to the mix: *Silky Underwear* (boasting a fresh forest scent), *All Girly* (smells like bubble gum), and

The Second Coming (I just like its name).

Using a tablespoon to mix the concoction until it's fully blended, I'm slightly troubled by the notion that I've inadvertently created a toxic combination that will aromatically poison my entire household, or maybe something potentially explosive. But nothing major happens when the perfumes are all combined, except a truly unusual odor (signature scent) rises from the tomato-sauce-stained bowl. I soak the tip of a cotton swab in the fragrant (pungent) blend and then dab it onto my wrists, the pulse points at the base of my throat, and then throwing caution to the wind, I stick my fingertips in and wipe them off on my clothes.

Yes, my signature scent, *Utter Breath of Earth's Girly Silky Second Coming*, is… is… I have not yet come up with a fitting descriptive term for it other than *fucker-nelly outrageous*.

Moving on….

* hair is the first thing a man will notice about you—rock thick sexy locks

Unfortunately, though, I have run out of time, as piles of AP Physics homework awaits me. Although men notice hair even before they notice breasts, according to the online article, I'm just going to have to make do with locks that are clean and shiny. Luckily, I have a special shampoo to ensure this.

So, before I head back to my mother's bathroom to subversively restock her closet with the three missing bottles of perfume I borrowed (stole), I glance again into the mirror at a blushing, red-lipped, sweet-smelling pirate with extremely ordinary, if not a hint too vivid, carrot orange hair.

And I wonder, is *this* the best version of myself? Is this the version of myself I want to be? Since I don't know the answers, I move on to my next question.

Will Jazz desire a sexily feminine Chance, a boyishly charming Chance, or no Chance at all, because he isn't gay?

I again come up empty.

Chapter 6
Not a Pie-stroll

It is ridiculously difficult to keep my lips a shiny red, my cheeks a softly blushing pink, my eyeliner unsmudged, and my signature scent freshly spritzed throughout a six-hour shift at a dirty farm stand. During my break, I find the porta-potty, reapply my Cherry Chapstick with a dab of clear gloss on top to improve the shine, and douse myself liberally with my signature scent, which I carry in my skinny jeans' cargo pocket in a Banana Schnapps nip bottle from my parents' liquor cabinet. My hope is that at the end of the workday, I'll bump into Jazz, and together we can stand by the soda machine out by the picnic tables near the parking lot, sip on sodas, and he can appreciate the red and pink shades of my face, drink in my enticing scent, admire my clean and shiny, but relatively normal, hair, and think, "Wow, Chance César is downright appealing!" in his simple country way.

Since it is my lucky day (um, not so much), as I make my way back to the barn, I'm confronted by a group of Fiske High School senior boys. The perfume and makeup that was feeling so right, suddenly feels like a very bad idea.

"What the fuck is that stench?" One of them asks as soon as we're within spitting (sniffing) distance of each other.

"Smells like Esmeralda the pig got loose from her cage and has been droppin' craps all over the fuckin' place." Yup. Eddie the Appalling, spewing his venom about my daring signature scent. The other four guys laugh like he's Adam Sandler doing stand-up.

I set my gaze on the rooster weathervane that's positioned on top of the barn. (I know, I know—Chance César is staring at a big cock. I've heard that one before, just sayin'.) And to steady my shot nerves, I imagine myself as I was on the runway at The Harvest Moon Festival, focused and fabulous. Placing one foot purposefully in front of the other, I force myself not to scramble like a skittish barn cat, but instead to walk with regal composure along this lonely path. Past four dudes who'd like nothing better than to see me cry.

"César, are you wearin' *makeup?*" It's Eddie again. Nothing gets past him, I swear. I realize at once that I should've gradually broken these assholes into the existence of my new beauty regime. Like, I probs should've let my shiny red lips sink into their brain cavities before they were forced to absorb the sight of my dark eyes outlined in jet black guyliner. But I'd been in this big freaking rush to show Jazz Donahue the best version of myself.

"Fuckin' right, dudes! The faggot's wearing makeup!"

Suddenly, I'm in the middle of a tight circle of guys who are closing in on me and squinting in an effort to get a load of my painted lips and eyes. "They sell eyeliner at the CVS Pharmacy downtown, if you guys are so frigging fascinated with it," my voice is haughty, but still I lift my right shoulder and turn my head toward it in an effort to casually wipe the gloss from my lips with my sweatshirt.

Another guy yells, "He's wearing lipstick! It's Ron Weasley in drag, and he's wearing lipstick!"

The douche bags all howl. I'm so glad I've made their day.

I try to shove my way out of the clusterfuck of assholes, but Eddie grabs my wrist and won't let go. "You forgot to paint your nails pink to go with your fairy sweatshirt, prissy-boy!"

He's right. I should have thought to do something with my fingernails, but that's beside the point. "Back off, redneck." I send him a nasty glare that is sufficiently potent to dissolve battery acid, and yank my hand away.

Interestingly, Appalling Eddie lets go of my wrist. And I know he desperately wants to give me hell, but he's just *a little bit* scared of me. Cuz I'm a loose cannon, and a certain Mr. Edwin Darling knows that I'm capable of doing just about anything when cornered. So wisely, he doesn't push me too far like he did that time last year when I completely lost it on him. I burst gracelessly through the circle of male bodies and make for the barn and the safety of my cash register.

"Hey don't run off all mad, little girl."

"Was it somethin' we said?"

"Nice sweatshirt, homo."

They cackle with evil laughter and I remind myself of two things. First, I will be graduating and getting out of this backwoods shithole in about eight months. And second, I have a plan, and a list, and a guy who I need to cajole into falling in love with me.

Keep your eyes on the prize, Chance.

***

I'm an honest diva, like I said before, and I'm sweating bullets as I stand by the soda machine, casually sipping a Dr. Pepper, and waiting for Jazz to pass by as he heads to his old Honda Accord—one of those used silvery-gray sedans that everyone and his mother drives. And I'm fully aware that I'm just as likely to come face-to-face once again with Eddie and his troupe of backwoods thugs, as I am with The Target. So, in short, I'm risking my ass for The Plan. For Jazz's true love. It had better freaking pay off.

And it's as if I wished him into being present, because all of a sudden Jazz is standing right in front of me.

He leans in toward me, and sniffs, long and deep. This is the moment of truth. "You smell real good, Chance." He looks directly at me, blinks once, and then closes his eyes and again inhales, by way of his nose, my *Utter Breath of Earth's Girly Silky Second Coming* fragrance.

Sha-blam! He might as well have told me he wants me to have his baby. I know I'm in like Flynn, which sounds a lot like something Emmy might say, but, oh, well. "I guess it's just me… you know, it's just the way I smell."

"It kinda makes me think of this time I went camping with the Boy Scouts in a forest way up in Maine, and somebody's dad brought these huge plastic pails of all different flavors of Bazooka Bubble Gum and… and we had these bubble blowing contests and… we chewed on that gum all weekend. So fun." He takes one more quick whiff and adds, "And I smell bananas."

I force a smile, thinking I really should have rinsed out the tiny Schnapps bottle before filling it with my signature scent. On the bright side, I'm impressed that Jazz is olfactorily tuned in enough to pick up on the subtle scents of *Silky Underwear and All Girly.* "Well, I'm not wearing cologne, or anything at all." I'm an above adequate liar when my back is against the wall. "Like I said, I guess it's just how I, um… how I naturally smell." I'm super glad I made a freakin' quart of the stuff.

His eyes widen and focus on my lips, just as they had during the "Gummy Bear Incident". I fight the urge to run my tongue over my teeth checking for unwanted food particles. Jazz would certainly think I was performing one of Emily's seductive lips/teeth/tongue motions and would probably run away into the night screaming. Instead I touch my mouth with my fingertips to insure that a portion of the Cherry Chapstick is still there, and mercifully, it is. I now know that Jazz is merely caught up in the fertile redness of my lips.

Our eyes meet. I am aware of my facial resemblance to Captain Jack Sparrow, and I take a moment to make a wish that Jazz is a fan of the *Pirates of the Caribbean* movies.

"And you look real nice tonight, Chance." He toes the dirt beneath his right work boot, but doesn't look away from my face. "You look sorta different… but different *good.*"

Double sha-blam! The Plan is working like a goddamn charm. That online ladies' magazine I swiped The List for The Plan from is going to receive a gushing thank-you note in their inbox tonight before I hit the hay.

And Jazz isn't finished with his compliments. "I mean, you look kinda pretty." If it had been a member of the thug gang who'd said that, I'd be totes pissed off, but Jazz's words are so very genuine. I have to struggle not to melt.

I glance down at my "Keep Calm and Kiss Boys" sweatshirt, wondering if he's referring to how the hot pink of the fabric brings out the subtle blushing of my cheekbones. But when I look back up, he's still staring into my eyes. Jazz's expression—soft and gentle, like a big tough biker dude looking at a roly-poly baby—makes me think of the thing I try hardest to ignore.

It makes me wonder if *Jazz* sees me as a girl, since I *am* smelling irresistibly sweet and painted to look pretty, and then... then I wonder if *I* see me as a girl.

#trueconfession: I used to let myself go there in my head. "There" being defined as the place in my mind that isn't sure which gender box I fit into, and is cool with that. Okay, so maybe last time I went there I was just a kid. Like, back before middle school was when I gave my brain the freedom to wonder. Since those days, though, I'd learned about the boxes—you have to be a boy or a girl, gay or straight, in the closet or out, masc or femme.

Pick a box, Chance, any box... Just pick one, for the love of Adam Lambert!

He's still looking at me, but I forget what he last said so there's no hope of me responding intelligently. Instead, I turn around and buy him a Coke. "Here, Jazz."

The thing is, I'm what you might call, caught in the middle. Well, not completely caught, cuz I know for a fact my body is male, and that I'm gay and, judging by my sweatshirt, I'm way far out of the closet. It's the rest of the gender stuff that wreaks havoc with my brain.

He smiles warmly. "Thanks." So maybe this time I *do* melt. And maybe his goofy crooked smile is making me turn as pink as my sweatshirt. What the hell—blushin' ain't a crime!

When I was a kid, I called myself a "pink boy." Other kids at school, even back then, called me a "girl-boy." Now, on the rare occasions I consider what has become such a touchy subject, I tell myself, "Chance you're just a dude in the 'middle space'." But to spell it out, I'm caught between genders.

And no, I have no freaking clue what to do with this concern, but still, when Jazz looks at me with that gentle expression, I wonder who he sees.

I wonder who I want him to see.

He breaks the silence with a truly clever line. "I like your sweatshirt."
HE LIKES MY FREAKING SWEATSHIRT!

My flippant response is automatic. "This old rag? I've had it for days!"

And then the weirdest thing happens. Right next to each other, we lean on the split-rail fence near the soda machine and we start to talk. We chat about school and movies and music like two regular dudes, not like a guy who has a plan and a guy who is The Target of The Plan.

It's super cool. But I will confess that in the back of my mind the entire time we are talking is a list of ten scientifically proven ways that I can make Jazz, not into my friend, but into my lover.

Which tactic will be number three?

Chapter 7
Copy Cat

I'm ready for this.

Last night I read up on all of the minute details regarding tactic number three (which is, on the official list, actually tactic number seven) of The Plan. In my bedroom I've practiced all of the appropriate kittenish behaviors on my stuffed rainbow-colored unicorn until he was giddy, not to mention as horny as hell. In addition, I conferred with my trusty Flirtation Coach (Emily).

And now I am ready.

I find that positive self-talk, including repetition of critical concepts, is helpful.

7. Try flirting... yes, tease him mercilessly.

It is what The Plan calls for. It is what I intend to do.

And I say this without so much as a trace of a glam smile.

This is serious business.

Point A. Initial engagement

I don't go to sit beside Jazz as has become my habit after I take my usual sip of water from the fountain on the back cafeteria wall. Instead, I sit alone, about three tables away from him, but directly in his line of vision. Which is critical. This is my starting point. For clarity, I have labeled it Point A.

I follow the article's instructions to a tee. The first thing I do is "get caught looking." One minute, my unsuspecting Target is chatting with Tessa McGill, and the next, he is locked in my spellbinding gaze. Once our gazes are fused, I start to initiate the practiced behaviors that will "stir up emotions he didn't know he had." Yeah, that's right—a direct quotation from the online article. And the choice to bat my eyelashes may sound trite, but it's scientifically proven that people blink faster when they're emotional. Batting my mascara-coated lashes at Jazz reveals my interest in him.

Jazzy-boy does a double take. It's as if he can't believe what's happening: Miss Harvest Moon, himself, is seated fifteen feet away, very blinkingly staring in his direction. And little does he know that my exercise in flirtation has only just begun. It's now time to unleash my "nervous excitement." I'm confident that this part of The Plan is gonna be a pie-stroll, but still, I follow the precise instructions, in the specific order that my Flirtation Coach demands.

Still staring, I tilt my head and bite down on my lower lip, immediately tasting the satisfying sweetness of cherries. I engage the slow smile and blush that were so successful on day one of The Plan. When I do this, Jazz's wide eyes bulge as if he's in pain, but I know better. He's just caught in my trap like a tiger by its tail.

The sparks are flying now. *Snap! Crackle! Pop!* Just like the online article promised.

This is everything!!

Point B. Secondary measures

I'm ready to move on to the secondary steps that will heighten our flirtatious connection. I rise slowly from my seat and saunter to Jazz's lunch table, making sure to sway my hips enticingly. His friends, I must say, are nearly as spellbound as he is. They stare up at moi, taking in my red lips, pink cheeks, lined eyes, and I'm sure they haven't missed my chalk white sweatshirt that informs them in bold lime green letters, "I kissed a boy and liked it."

"You smell good," Tessa offers, her voice tentative. I *think* she's trying to be friendly, but I'm a harsh judge of character, having been burned too many times to count.

"Yes, I know."

Her eyes go all round at my curt reply, but I haven't time to dwell on that because I know that things are about to start getting technical here, and it's gonna unfold fast. Cuz here's where I express myself with body language.

I slip into the empty spot beside Jazz and point my knees toward him, per the specific requirements of The Plan. I'm careful not to fold my arms, which would create an emotional barrier, and then I make my move—I lean against his arm. I swear he gasps at the shock of our first moment of physical contact, but who wouldn't? Fiske High School's only makeup-wearing, flamboyant queer kid is glued to his left shoulder.

"Dude." He says in a low voice, sitting up straighter. "S'up?"

One, two, three... I correct my slumping posture, as well. "The sun, I guess. That's what's s'up." (Incidentally, I've moved on to **Point C—Imitation.**)

Puzzled, probs by everything about Chance César, both of his friends turn to look at *him*, not me. Interesting.

"You want a couple French fries, Chance? They gave me almost a bucketful today." Jazz is also very generous. I'm growing more smitten by the minute.

I nod. He pushes the tray with the plate of fries on it toward me, but I don't reach for one until just after he does.

One, two, three... I snatch a fry and dip it in the small pool of ketchup on the side of the plastic plate, swirling an S shape *exactly* as Jazz did, and then I pop it between my shiny red lips.

"It's so cool that you got this lunch block, Chance, so you and me, and these guys, too, can all hang out." Kyle and Tessa glance at me and shrug. "But how come ya never buy lunch?"

Well, that would be because I get my lunch at the salad bar with Emily in my real lunch block an hour from now.

"Light eater," I lie.

Jazz picks up another French fry, swirls it, and down the hatch it goes.

One, two, three... My turn.

He watches as I feed myself the French fry, and tilts his head to the left, like he's trying to figure something out. I suspect that I might need to be less obvious in my mimicry. But still, I tilt my head to the left, at the very same angle as The Target.

"So you goin' to the football game this Saturday?"

"This Saturday," I echo. I have resolved to never attend another football game in my high school career. But in the interest of mimicry, I say, *"This Saturday* there's a *football game.* Hmmm."

Jazz wipes his mouth with the back of his hand. *One, two, three...* I wipe mine with a napkin (force of habit). He stretches his arms wide. *One, two, three...* I stretch a tad more delicately. He twiddles his thumbs slowly. *One two three... I twiddle—well,* enough said.

I am Jazz Donahue's mirror. We are exact replicas of each other. Anyone with functioning eyeballs can see it.

To be real, everyone *can* see it—his two BFFs aren't the only people who are gawking at us in what I'd call a curified fascination. (*Curified* is the unique combination of *curious* and *horrified.* And yes, *I* coined the expression.)

Jazz shifts on his seat and then goes for it. He stands up and sits down very quickly. I know he's testing me.

One two three... yes, like a bold of lightening, I'm up and down as well.

Can you say copycat?

Incidentally, everybody knows that imitation is the most sincere form of flattery, right?

I believe the deal is sealed and so I actually slide a notecard that I've doused with heavy portions of my signature scent, across the table, my cell phone number written coyly up in its top right-hand corner. And though he picks it up and holds it to his nose, all the while until the lunch bell rings we sit beside each other in a sort of expectant silence—my knees pointed his way, and Jazz, chin in hands, notecard at nostrils, staring directly across the table at Tessa. As if she can help him.

That's when it hits me, and it hits me like a rolling pin to the side of the head. Jazz isn't smiling and laughing and basking in the afterglow of my mimicry. No—he is staring at Tessa McGill, uncomfortable as a fat pig at a butcher shop, and wishing fervently for his lunch block to come to a speedy conclusion.

I may have sealed the deal in proving how similar we are, but I suddenly realize that Jazz still hasn't warmed up to my advances. His reciprocation has been limited to a wary smile and an offer of French fries.

The Plan may not be working as well as I had originally thought.

Curses....

Chapter 8
Keep Things Spicy

Tonight we are at Emily's house and here, there are well-established rules for when we are in her bedroom alone. It appears that *her mother* views me as more of a boy than a girl.

* Bedroom door stays open at all times.
* Emily hangs out/sleeps on her bed—alone—while Chance César interacts with BFF from the loveseat in the room's far corner.
* No food in the bedrooms—Mrs. Benson has an almost debilitating phobia of ants.
* No loud music, laughter, or "carrying on" after ten p.m.

Nothing truly restrictive. But it's eleven o'clock and we're trying to hold a private conversation in hushed late-night tones, Emmy on her bed and moi across the room on the stiff loveseat. And despite the hushed tones and the exaggerated distance, I can easily see that Emily isn't her usual quirky self.

"Dish, girlfriend." It is nothing short of a demand. In my defense, I can't relax when my best girl isn't chill. "Tell Channy your problems."

She shakes her head. "Not yet. Let's focus on The Plan for a while."

"Oh, puh-lease… your problems are my problems, hunny." I would grasp Emmy's hand and squeeze it if I wasn't banished across the room from her. "Now, spill it."

She ignores my plea. "You didn't leave Jasper with the impression that you are *high maintenance,* did you?"

"No, of course not." That would be a cardinal sin, according to the Today's Lady online article. I take this opportunity to practice my best *resting bitch face.* I must never allow myself to appear overly sweet and unsuspecting. "What do you take me for, a novice?"

"You *are* a novice, Channy." Deciding to break the non-fraternization law set up by her mother, she hops off the bed, crosses the room, and joins me on the loveseat. "And though The Target must consider you hot and sexy and alluring, giving the appearance that you are high maintenance is the kiss of death for a relationship."

"No, he has no idea of the amount of time I spent in the porta-potty… um, 'freshening up'."

"Maybe he's not even gay—ever consider that?"

"Um, *hello*! Of course that possibility has crossed my mind a time or two or ten thousand." I smirk at Em because, in truth, I have as little clue if Jazz is gay as I have about whether I am an inner boy or girl. But it would certainly make the success of The Plan more of a challenge if Jazz were straight as a ruler. I mirror Emily's nervous finger tapping on her other knee, as I admit, "I may have overdone it in the mimicry department." Maybe I was a chimpanzee in a past life. "Monkey see, monkey do, right?"

"You might be right about that."

Now *I'm* bewildered.

"Lemur lovers sync their scents. If Jasper comes to school smelling like *Utter Breath of Earth's Girly Silky Second Coming* fragrance, you know you're making progress."

"How do you even know that—you know, about lemurs?"

She ignores my last question, so I chalk her abundant knowledge of lemur behavior up to the fact that before she met me her only friends were books. "I think it's time to spice things up. And according to the article, men can't resist mystery."

Deciding I'm gonna proceed with the assumption that Jazz is gay, I grab my laptop off of the side table and open it to The List for The Plan. "That sounds like number six."

6. Be a little mysterious—you are different from the rest.

Okaaaayyyy... calling me "different from the rest" is truly quite an understatement. Proving it to Jazz shouldn't be too challenging at all. In other words, it should be one fucker-nelly of a pie-stroll.

"Let's look at the details," I suggest before I get overly confident.

"Let's, shall we?" Emmy is all business, and I swear I will find out whatever it is that's troubling her before the night is over. But for now we lean in together and read number six's details.

* don't tell him your whole life story—let him wonder
* keep things spicy in the bedroom
* show him the other side of you
* make him laugh
* surprise him

Emmy and I look at each other and blink at the same time.

"Spicy in the bedroom?" A panicky feeling overcomes me for a multitude of reasons. "I've never even been alone with him."

"Maybe you should put that one on hold for now."

"Yeah, maybe I should." I sigh with relief. "I think number six is gonna be the most difficult one so far."

We're quiet for a minute. Then Em smiles and says, "A dooza-palooza, for sure."

I sniff, knowing this new word has been introduced at just this moment to lighten my load. "Why don't you try telling me about the dooza-palooza in *your* life? Because no matter how much you avoid it, girlfriend, I know you better than anybody else. And you are wigging out about—well, tell me, why don't ya?"

And just like that, her eyes fill with tears and she leans toward me to break yet another of her mother's non-fraternization rules. We hug and she holds me against her for a long time. "You know how so much as the mention of the J-word can make me bawl?" She queries directly into my left ear.

Yeah, I know that the mere utterance of the word *Juilliard* is capable of bringing my BFF to her knees. "Like a baby with diaper rash *and* an empty milk bottle," I reply directly into her right ear, which happens to be conveniently pressed against my lips. I don't know much about babies, but I figure a sore butt and an empty belly would bring one of them to tears. For the past year, if not more, Emily's desire to attend The Juilliard School as a Drama Division major has brought no shortage of tears of longing and anxiety. "So what's got you so emo right now, girlfriend?"

Emmy lets me go and I see those tears dripping down her face, which is unacceptable to me. "It's the fucker-nelly essay and...."

I wait for her to finish.

"You know, the application essay just matters so much. Every time I start to write, my mind goes blank. I mean, there's *nada* in the noggin, Channy. I'm absolutely empty!"

"That *is* a dooza-palooza."

She sighs again. "And then there's... there's another problem."

"Well, don't clam up *now*, bestie."

She lifts her sleep shirt and grabs a hold of her rounded belly. "They aren't gonna want me with this."

A fire lights up inside my heart and suddenly I'm pissed off. My BFF is beautiful. Perfect. She is as she was meant to be. And yes, Emily has confided her insecurity about her weight to me before—this feeling is nothing new for her. I've often told her to forget what society thinks, but then I also struggle with not being as I'm expected to be by the world. In fact, I constantly wonder why the hell I can't be just a plain old gay guy. Why do I have to be this guy in the "middle space"?

A boy without a box.

But this is about Emily right now.

"Your belly is part of you. The Juilliard School will be lucky to have you and your belly and your butt and all of your insecurities and your made-up words and—like, all of you." Emmy bites her bottom lip, wanting so badly to believe what I'm saying, but not at all convinced. "Let's look at the essay question, kkkk?"

Emily shoots to her feet, trots to her bed, and grabs her laptop. She flops back on the pillows and opens it up, appearing relieved to have her problem out in the open and to be dealing with it directly. And I finally am able to exhale because her relief is my relief. "The essay's purpose is to get a picture of me beyond what my application says. So I'm supposed to write about why I've chosen to be an actor and what my personal goals are." She is focused now. "They want to know my passions and my politics and about the people who matter to me and...."

Dooza-paloozas. We all have them, I guess. My dooza-palooza isn't so much how to make Jasper Donahue fall in love with me, though it's a subject well worth focusing my overly active mind on. My true dooza-palooza is figuring out my gender box.

After discussing options for her Juilliard application essay until well past midnight, I turn onto my side and curl up into what probably resembles a fetal ball on the loveseat in the corner. But my fine ass hangs over the edge into midair, which is not remotely comfortable. I shift around in an attempt to find a position on a loveseat that works for my long legs.

I don't know why I care about the whole gender thing so much. It's like, I just do. And since I met Jazz I've been basically obsessing 24/7 as to whether I feel more like a guy or a girl. Cuz "chances are" he doesn't fall asleep and dream about a dude who's stuck in the gray area between girl and boy.

#trueconfession: I want Jazz to notice me and to fall for me—I just don't know if he wants Channy, the femme, or Chance, the butch. Maybe if I knew what he wanted me to be it would help me figure out what I am.

I finally give up on the cramped loveseat, grab my pillow and blanket, and drop down to the floor. At least I can stretch out here. And thankfully, Emily's room is carpeted. In a cornflower blue velvet plush, which I must say, is quite sleep-inducing.

Before I fall asleep, I force myself to draw a conclusion in regard to my own dooza-palooza. But first, I stifle a yawn and admit that the specifics of what *I* actually want to be in terms of gender just seem so blurry right now. The thing I really know for totes sure is that I want to be a concrete *something*—a boy *or* a girl I can present to Jazz and say, "This is what I am. Are you into me?"

"Run that by me again, Channy?" Emmy asks through a yawn.

Had I said that out loud? I need to get a grip. "I'm gonna crash now, doll. I was just saying nighty-night."

Chapter 9
A Man of Mystery

This is the perfect opportunity to allow Jazz to see the other side of me.

Tonight is the Fiske High School Corn Maze Challenge for Charity. About twenty high school kids who are in the market for fast and easy volunteer hours to put on their college applications have shown up at the Beans and Greens cornfield to run a charity event in which we escort small groups of kids through the corn maze and then fill them up on hot apple cider and candy corn when they finally find their way to the end. I'm one of the escorts, as is Jazz. We run into each other in the maze about ten times as we try to get our small groups through, and each time he's friendly and seems happy to see me. At one point he introduces me to this cute little brown-haired girl, his seven-year-old sister JoJo, who's in his group. He calls her his assistant, which makes her grin. It's dang cute and I find my crush on him intensifying. As if that's possible.

At the end of the maze, the high school students wait with the small groups as their parents come to pick them up. I roughhouse with my gang of six-year-olds in the grass in front of the cider stand. I let them feed me candy corn with their dirty fingers. I even let them mess up my hair, which is a true sacrifice. By the time all of my kids are gone I'm a dirty mess, and I suspect I'm far from being "the best version of myself" called for in the online article.

"Chance! Hey, Chance, over here!" Jazz is waving at me with both arms, in SOS mode.

I walk to where he sits on the cold grass watching JoJo play tag with her friends in the dim light of the strategically placed lanterns, and I kneel down beside him. "Hi, Jazz."

He reaches up and rubs my right cheek. "Got dirt on ya." Well, the article said to show him my less-than-ladylike side, as in "get some dirt on your hands." I guess dirt on my face qualifies. "Can you talk for a while?"

Number six: be a little mysterious….

I hesitate before answering. Keeping someone waiting provides suspense, if nothing else. "Well…" I examine my dirty fingernails and try not to grimace, "I suppose I can visit with you for a minute."

An odd, maybe injured, look crosses Jazz's face at my response, but it quickly passes. In the dark evening, draped in shadows, he looks handsome and rugged and mysterious. I can only hope that the shadows are doing the same favors for me… however, I highly doubt it with regard to the rugged part. "You here alone tonight, Chance? Aren't you usually always with that girl, Emily Benson? The one who's in all the plays?"

Don't give it all away, Chance. You are not an open book.

"Yeah, I spend a sizeable portion of my free time with Emily." A very noncommittal response. Ten points for moi.

Again, Jazz appears stymied by my reply, but still he makes another attempt at engaging me. "So, you live by the apple pickin' farm?"

"In that general vicinity." A very intriguing reply, hmm?

"You're an only child, right?"

"I guess you could say that."

He regards me with an expression that can best be categorized as "huh?" I casually check my front teeth for unwanted pieces of candy corn with my tongue, but I'm sure not to turn it into one of those sexy mouth movements that would probably make things slightly more intriguing than either of us is ready for. Then JoJo runs to Jazz and dives on top of him. Her two friends join in.

What have I got to lose? YOLO, right? Time to surprise him.

That's when I jump onto the pig pile. The girls love it. The sound of giggling suffuses the chilly night air and within a couple of seconds I hear the deeper, smoother sound of Jazz's laughter. But soon, the girls, like a playful pile of puppies, roll off us and are on to other adventures. When I get back on my knees, I catch a glimpse of Jazz, and he's studying me, his eyes round. He can't for the life of him figure me out.

Cha-ching! I have succeeded in being unpredictable as all get-out.

"Didn't expect that of you, dude." He speaks slowly.

"Didn't expect what?" Yes, I am innocence personified.

"The pig pile thing… it was *so cool.*"

Yaaasss! Number six is working. I am an official man of mystery—not a "clone of all the other girls." Pleased by my conclusion, I smile, but I do so with *only* the right side of my mouth. That'll certainly make him wonder.

At this point, I figure Jazz should be sufficiently titillated by my irresistible un-clone-like behavior. I wait, like a full five minutes, for him to make a move—to lean over and grab my hand, or to ask me for a date. But, as Emily says… *nada.* Nothing. We just sit there in this pleasant—and very platonic—silence.

It's almost ten at night. I'm tired, filthy—I even have dirt in my goddamn mouth—and my signature scent is history. I've just about had it. I've done everything strictly by the book (online article) to make him fall head over work boots for moi. I've smiled right to my freaking eyeballs and been flirtatious enough for him to catch a social disease from me if I had one. Not to mention that I've been *incredibly* attractive, if I do say so myself, as well as the definition of intriguing. This shit isn't working.

Jazz probably has no interest in dating a she-he with a major identity crisis and candy in his teeth.

"This face leaves at ten o'clock. And I'm on it." I announce in my best bitchy tone and then I stand up, flick my wrist, and strut away without a backward glance.

Sha-blam! And not in a good way.

Chapter 10
Dream On

Had a dream about that super suck-ola night last fall. It happens every once in a while, usually when I'm stressed about another matter, entirely. And tonight, when I went to bed, it felt like life totes sucked to the max because I was super-mega-ultra-waaaay frustrated with Jazz's complete lack of interest in the amazing moi.

Jazz is probably not even gay and I'm deluding myself. Wouldn't be the first time. So at midnight, I went to bed angry and I dreamed about the time I deluded myself, with the indispensable assistance of Eddie the Appalling, at a Fiske High School football game. To be specific, it was during halftime at last year's final home FHS football game.

Football and Edwin—my least favorite combination. Give me beans and rice, any day.

I'm a sucker. Any gay high school junior who voluntarily meets a giant homophobic asshole under the bleachers at halftime of a home football game to "find out who's been lusting after ya" surely qualifies as an elite Grade A Sucker. In my defense, I'm a lonely sucker, and if a random guy is supposedly lusting after me—hell, if a dude even thinks my ass looks cute in skinny jeans—I want to know who he is.

But as I should have expected, the only people under the bleachers when I arrive are Eddie the Appalling and his gang of backwoods thugs, none of whom is lusting for Chance César's fine ass. They are, however, lusting for a fight.

It isn't much of a fight. It starts with the usual taunting. Eddie calls me a pussy, a faggot, a homo. I say something along the lines of "if I wanted to hear from an asshole, I'd fart," which very predictably pisses Eddie off, and presents an opportunity for his dumbass sidekicks to rile him up further. Edwin feeds me his fist, time and again. I spit out a mouthful of blood, and then... and then I lose it. As in, totes.

I'm talking about a humongous freak-out hissy fit. Suddenly, I'm a stray feral cat on steroids and a douche bag is trying to trap me—I'm clawing, kicking, hissing, and possibly biting—my memory of the exact retaliatory measures I employed fails me. Fear fuels my anger, which in turn, fuels this intolerable sense of helplessness that again fuels my fear. It's a vicious cycle, and by the time the vice principal and the assistant football coach show up on the scene, Edwin Darling is as bloody and messed up as I am.

We're dragged away to separate locations in the school, and take turns getting cleaned up in the nurse's office. Then we're both condemned to three-day suspensions for fighting on school grounds.

End result: With regard to Edwin the Appalling and his associates, I must live in The Land of Anxious Anticipation. I'm not so much afraid, in the classic sense, as I dread the drama of a repeat performance. Fighting for your life, even when reasonably successful, takes a toll on a person. But for the most part the student body keeps their distance from Chance César. They tease me, they laugh at me—I'm the butt of a multitude of jokes. But there are limits to the torment. The assholes keep a safe distance from me because nobody wants to be on the wrong side of a vicious catfight.

Well, I don't need to dwell on that shit anymore, so I go downstairs. When I was a kid and I'd had a bad dream, I would go climb in bed with my parents. But if I'm gonna be real, I'll admit doing that never helped much. Mom always said I could stay for five minutes and then she actually set the timer on her phone, and when it beeped I had to leave. Lying there in her bed, I never relaxed. I counted the seconds 'til it was time to split, and then I shuffled back to my room feeling lonelier and more miserable than I had before.

So maybe Mom has never been what you could call a warm, fuzzy lady. And believe it or not, I'm cool with her "hands off" parenting style, for the most part. Cuz it made me stronger. I learned hard lessons, and I learned them young.

#lifelessonnumberone: Figure out how to comfort yourself, Chance.

Which involves Cheez-Its. Cheez-Its are mandatorbs to self-soothing.

I go into the kitchen in search of them. Although my mother isn't overly tuned into me in the emo department, she's plugged in when it comes to things like knowing we should always have Cheez-Its. Maybe she's figured out that they're a self-soothing requirement for me, and she'd prefer to spend her time at the grocery store buying junk food for her melodramatic son than actually discussing his problems with him. Whatever.

I sit down at the granite-topped counter grasping my box of cracker-tranquilizers like it can save me, pop it open, stuff a small handful into my mouth.

Time for the whole *obsessive ingenious overthinking* thing that I'm so good at.

What it comes down to, if I can momentarily set aside the less than minor gender quandary I suffer with, is that I detest feeling powerless in my non-relationship with Jasper Donahue. I've frigging broken my ass to make

him stand up and take notice of yours truly, and he just sits there and stares.
Powerlessness sucks donkey balls.

The List for The Plan… which number will return the power to me?

I scan my mental list and number four stands out as the WTG at this juncture.

4. Leave him wanting more—absence makes the heart grow fonder.

This I can do, and it will be a pie-stroll.

Chapter 11
The Thrill of the Chase

I stroll past Jazz's lunch table, apparently not noticing how amazing he looks today in the thin white T-shirt that shows off his pecs in just the right way, snug jeans, and work boots.(*As if I'd miss that eye candy.*). I take a nice long sip of water from the fountain, directing my backside—which Emmy says looks superhot in these butt-hugging high-water khakis—at The Target.

Wanting me much? I think it so loud that Jazz can probs hear.

In any case, he's sitting alone today. As I walk in, I check to see if he's looking around to see who's noticing me noticing him, because staring at yours truly's ass is dangerous to your social status. But he isn't looking all around. He's totally focused on moi.

I can feel his eyes on me—not so much on my backside, as just on me, in general. So maybe I wiggle my backside just a tad (ass-wiggling ain't a crime) as I stand back up, spin around, and head for the exit. I do the America's Next Top Model runway strut right past him, and then I glance back cagily to see if he's still watching me. Which he is. And he appears puzzled. Side note: Jazz probs thinks I have a total thing for this out-of-the-way water fountain. *Hehehe.*

"Hey! Chance—why you in such a hurry?" He sounds eager. "Take a load off and come sit down with me."

I'm almost all the way past him, but I stop, take a step back, and stand casually just off the far edge of his lunch table. And I'm coy. "How are you doing today, Jazzy?"

"Doin' good. Too bad you had to leave so quick Saturday night. Was gonna see if ya needed a ride home."

"I had my own car. No need to put yourself out."

I'm getting used to receiving these perplexed looks from Jazz. Right now, though, his expression seems confused, but also hurt, so I slide in beside him at the lunch table. I pride myself in not being mean.

"My little sister—remember JoJo—she had a blast at the corn maze."

"The kids in my group were into it too."

"JoJo thought you were so cool when you jumped into the pile of kids. She laughed about it all the way home."

"Well, your little sister is adorbs. Just like her big bro."

He blushes sweetly, and I want to stay at this lunch table with Jazz Donahue for the rest of my life, no joke. We slip into easy conversation about

51

how Beans and Greens is closing for the season and our roles in shutting down the farm, and I have to keep reminding myself that he'll want me more if I say goodbye while this conversation is still interesting.

* create demand by limiting supply—of yourself

"Well, I have to make tracks, got an appointment with my Econ book."
And just like I always fantasize about, he places his hand on my arm. "Stay for the rest of lunch, I wanna talk to you more."
Make him work for it, César. Let him fight for what he wants.
"Nah, I really have to head out."

* being easy won't make him go crazy

I want him to go crazy for me so badly I can taste it so *I have* to walk away before he's ready for me to go. This "getting Jazz to fall in love with me" thing is hard werk. But now it's Jazz's turn to learn the meaning of "werk it." He looks up at me with sad, "please don't go" puppy dog eyes.

"I'm out." Leaving him there is as hard as licking my elbow. But I do it—leave, not lick my elbow. I will allow Jazz to experience the thrill of the chase. But I will say, it probably hurts me more than it hurts him.

***

IT WERKED!! OMG!! IT WERKED!!
I am the king… no, the queen… or whatever the case, I am make-him-earn-it ROYALTY!!

It's a freaking fact—absence really *does* make the heart grow fonder! I know this because of the phone call I just received.

Still wearing my silky robe, I sink down into my soft sheets. And I smile because there's everything in the world to smile about. Jazz Donahue just called and asked if I want to hang out at his house on Friday night. And although the online article suggests I yawn, excuse myself politely, and then accept the offer with cool apathy, I was like, "Hell, yeah! Where do you want me, and when?"

Jazz seemed a bit apologetic when he explained that we'd be watching his sister cuz his mom has to work late at her second job, but having JoJo there doesn't lessen my excitement even slightly. She's a cute kid and I think little girls are tons of fun—so much so that part of me has always longed to be one—and her big brother is, as Emmy would say in her retro-speak, "a total dreamboat."

I resolve to write yet another prolific letter of gratitude to Today's Lady Online Magazine before I go to sleep tonight.

So pumped. *Squeeeee*....

Chapter 12
"Do you really wanna go there?"

Unlike the fake lunch block that I spend every day with Jazz, my *real* lunch block with Emily has been a total bitch lately. I can't say who the major target of the bullshit is—Emmy or me—as neither of us has a sizeable fan club at Fiske High School. But I will say that the front table by the salad bar is a cold place to be, and that's not just because of the draft that comes in from the hallway.

"Nice makeup, girl-boy." It seems Edwin hasn't forgotten my nickname from grade school, which sucks for me.

But this diva never backs down. "Thanks. Haven't you heard—I was the head makeup artist on *Evita?*"

"Eh-what-uh?" Eddie the Appalling wrinkles his greasy forehead and runs his hand over his buzz-cut hair. Clearly, he is unfamiliar with Tony Award winning Broadway musicals. Not that I'm shocked. He quickly shifts his attention to Emily. "How do you put up with him, fat-ass?"

My BFF isn't as good as I am at deflecting evil taunts. She looks up at him with wide eyes and seems to lose her appetite, pushing her salad toward the middle of the table.

"Oh, that's cold, my darling Eddie." (See what I did with his name, there? Clever, I know.) I stand up. "I wouldn't go there if I were you." I then "rawr" at him like a ticked-off tigress, throwing in a clawing gesture to get my point across. "Do you *really* wanna go there?"

I can tell by the look on his face that he's remembering how long it took for the scratches to heal after our last entanglement.

"I personally could live without going there, but you know me—I'm impulsive as hell." I fold my arms across my chest and thrust out my right hip. "Piss me off and I'm likely to do abso-fucking-lutely anything."

The bulk of my attention is focused on my adversary, but it's impossible to miss that we've gathered an audience. An audience of indifferent "watchers"—the multitudes of apathetic teens who will later text each other, "did you see the homo and the bully go head-to-head at lunch today?" They don't matter one smidgeon in the scheme of things, but my Emily does.

At this point, Eddie and I are eye-to-eye and chest-to-chest. Lucky for him, one of his thugs bails him out. "Get too close to that fag and you'll get AIDS—am I wrong?" The big oaf grabs Eddie by the arm and pulls him away.

But he doesn't remove his gaze from mine. "You better watch out when

we're off school grounds, pansy."
   If I said I didn't shudder, I'd be lying.

Chapter 13
First Date?

I put what you might call mega-supreme effort into choosing my outfit for tonight. End result: I look kinda fab—thankfully, not so much *ratchet*, although I *am* rocking mean side bangs. Torn black jeggings, an oversized baby pink hoodie that says, *Real Men Wear Pink*, and my bubblegum-colored Chuck Taylors. I've applied just a touch of guyliner but I was liberal with the Cherry Chapstick.

Overall effect? I'm sufficiently fetching to meet the Queen of England. Which just so happens to be on my bucket list.

When I get to Jazz's place, I park the car, pinch my cheeks, and momentarily wonder if I should have gone for a more sophisticated look—like maybe a silky gray button-down shirt and black pointy-toed boots, my hair thrown up in a casual man-bun. But it's too late for that, now. I get out of the car and stand in front of Jazz's apartment building.

Pop, shrug, and stare… first things first.

I climb the stairs.

Is this a date? Or is it just two dudes hanging out?

I knock five times.

Seems like the right number of knocks.

I stop and wait.

The door swings open and I'm presented with the tear-filled eyes of a familiar little brown-haired girl. "Hiya… J-Jazz told me to answer the door." She sucks in a deep wobbly breath. "C-cuz he's cleaning up the nail polish." Her next breath seems to cause her entire chest to swell up. And then she releases a sob.

"Hey, kid, what's the matter?"

"I sp-spilled all of the… the *Orange-Orange* nail polish… o-on the living r-room rug."

"That *is* a disaster, truly." I speculate on whether she's upset that the *Orange-Orange* polish is now gone or that it made a mess on the rug. I make my best guess. "Do you have a lemon-yellow nail polish and a cherry red, cuz if you do, I can make you *JoJo Takes a Chance Orange* polish. I've done it before."

"*Jojo Takes a Chance Orange* nail polish?" She examines me quite skeptically while tugging on one tiny pigtail. "Why the 'takes a chance' part?"

"Cuz my name is Chance, and if you give me a chance I think I can make you a color that's better than *Orange-Orange*. I'll make you a color that's even better than my hair!" *Okaaaayyyy*... so maybe my claim is a slight exaggeration cuz my tangerine locks totes rock, but I'll say *anything* to stop her tears.

With that, JoJo takes my hand and pulls me urgently down the hall.

In the living room, Jazz is on his knees, bent over a wet spot on the floor, scrubbing with a Hello Kitty toothbrush. He looks up at me. "I told JoJo to let you in. I'm busy trying to put an end to a crisis."

I step closer to look down at the spot he is scrubbing on the gray rug, thinking that I have the very same toothbrush hanging in my bathroom at home. *Okaaaaay*... so maybe I don't miss the way his biceps tighten up with his effort. "I think you got the stain up."

Jazz nods. "Problem is, we don't have no more... um... bunches of oranges nail polish, or whatever, and I think JoJo's heart mighta' been set on it." He looks desperate. "Don't spaz, Jo. I can paint your nails blue. You like blue, right?"

I turn to JoJo, who just so happens to be glaring at her brother. "It's almost Halloween, Jasper! *Blue won't work!*"

Time to step in and save a couple of asses. "Go get your nail polish—you have red and yellow, right?"

The girl nods at me seriously.

"And if you have any gold tones with glitter, or even shiny silver, grab them too. And a plastic cup, if you have one, and a couple of toothpicks."

She runs off to do my bidding, and I call after her, "Bring clear polish, too! A topcoat is the secret to a lasting manicure!"

Finally Jazz stands up, still looking down at the wet spot on the rug. "Whatcha gonna do, Chance?"

"I'm gonna save the day." Jazz looks bewildered, so I add more slowly, "I'm going to give JoJo a manicure."

For the next hour, I occupy myself with blending various polishes together in a tiny paper cup, helping JoJo stir it up with toothpicks until we have the perfect shade of orange, and finally painting the her fingernails *JoJo Takes a Chance Orange.* Jazz sits beside us on the floor as we work on the coffee table. He's very quiet and keeps looking back and forth from JoJo to me.

When I'm finished, JoJo stands up, spins around twice, and fans her fingers out in front of her. "This color is way better than *Orange-Orange!* This color is so... so glittery!" She prances around their very plain living room and it looks like so much fun I'm tempted to join in. "*JoJo Takes a Chance Orange* is the best color in the world!"

"Try the universe, hunny." I wink at her.

Jazz appears more baffled than usual, but he still manages to instruct his sister, "Well, don't mess it up, Jo. Sit down on the couch and stay still," he hands her the remote, "and watch them Dalmatians 'til I fix ya supper." He sneaks a glance at me. "You can watch *101 Dalmatians* with JoJo, if ya feel like it. She's kind of obsessed by Cruella de Vil these days."

Although I have my own private obsession with Cruella de Vil, I shake my head and follow Jazz into the kitchen.

"Was thinkin' maybe I'd make pizza tonight." His face suddenly turns pink and it hits me that he's embarrassed.

"Can I help you with it?" Make-your-own-dinner-night is nothing new to me. Jazz's face grows still brighter—its hue now approaches a very appealing fuchsia that brings to mind pink Starbursts, which everyone knows are the best ones. (Sorry, yellow Starbursts.)

"Hangin' out here can't be no fun for you. I bet you wish you didn't even come over."

I send him a baffled glance of my own, which is a first. "I was thinking pretty much the exact opposite of what you just said."

"Chance, you got all dressed up nice, and ya smell real good, and ya came here, probably thinkin' we'd watch a movie that's rated R and get take-out Chinese, or something cool like that. But you get here and get stuck paintin' a little girl's nails, then you have to eat homemade pizza and watch *101 Dalmatians*."

"I want to eat homemade pizza."

"Dunno why."

To be candid or not to be candid, that is the question.
Don't give it all away, Chance, you are so-o-o not an open book.
But... but Jazz looks so sad.

"Jazz, usually I eat take-out food alone in my bedroom. Believe me, eating homemade pizza with you and JoJo will be a treat."

Jazz is so easy to read. He tilts his head and studies me, probs wondering why I eat my meals alone in my room. "'Kay."

He grabs the ingredients out of the refrigerator and I take the canister of flour off the counter. "Where are we gonna put the pizza together?"

"Over here." He balances everything just barely long enough to plunk it all down on the kitchen table. "Table's clean. You can drop a pile of flour on it."

I dust a bit of flour on the table with my fingers as Jazz turns on the oven. He comes back with a round pizza pan. "So where's your mom?"

Taking the dough out of the package, he mumbles, "Working."

"At night?"

"During the school year, she works Monday to Friday, days, plus like five nights a week."

I take the dough from his hands and start to press it onto the flour-covered table, hoping there's no nail polish left on my fingers. "Got a glass so I can roll it out?"

"Better, I got a rolling pin." He gets the rolling pin from a drawer, and hands it to me with a wink. I roll out the dough.

"Why does she work so much? She a major career lady? That's how my 'rents are." I hope I'm not being too intrusive, but inquiring minds want to know.

He chuckles. "Shit, no. It's called making ends meet." He drags the flattened dough onto the pan. "Mom makes minimum wage at the Walmart by the mall. So she's gotta wait tables at night."

I totes can't relate. My parents are workaholics because they love what they do. They thrive on it—eat it, sleep it, and even dream it, probs. I sigh.

"That's why I go to vocational training. Gonna be an electrician. Never gonna wonder where the cash for our rent is coming from like my mom has to do."

"I get that."

"So, I'm mostly in charge of keeping the apartment cleanish, y' know, and doing laundry and stuff like that."

"Like taking care of JoJo?"

Jazz holds out the jar of sauce and a spoon to see if I want to do the honors. And I do. "Yeah, I'm in charge of JoJo most of the time." He looks at me as if to see if I'm okay with it.

"Cool." And I *am* okay with it. I think it's cool because he and his mom and his sister are a family, and by working together they act like one. "You wanna sprinkle the cheese?"

He nods. "Gotta go light on JoJo's part. She won't eat it if it's too cheesy—says it chokes her." I again fixate on the muscles of his upper arms as he sprinkles the cheese. (Last time I checked, bicep appreciation was *not* a crime.) "I'll pop it in the oven and set the timer. Chow time'll be in 'bout sixteen minutes."

***

It's so cray sitting down at a kitchen table and eating dinner like I'm part of this family. Like I actually belong here. We do the traditional "how was your day, dear?" shit with JoJo, and she's all about answering every question. It seems that the young lady created a poetic ode to cupcakes in writing, read aloud from a book about a lonely dinosaur in reading, and learned how to make change for a dollar in math. Her fave part of the school day is recess, though, cuz she gets a chance to chase the boys.

She tells us she usually catches them. I tell her I'm envious.

After dinner, it's about nine o'clock, and Jazz helps JoJo change into her nighty, of which I'm also envious because the shade of purple is simply divine. After she says goodnight to me, I wait in the living room while Jazz puts her to bed.

The honest diva part of me will admit my heart is pounding like I'm a bride-to-be, third in line at the annual Filene's Basement wedding gown sale.

Am I gonna get my first kiss tonight?

I pull the Cherry Chapstick out of my jeggings back pocket, which is no small task cuz they're tighter than a snake's skin, and I smear it liberally on my lips.

"Hey, dude." Jazz saunters into the living room. He looks tired and maybe a tad awkward. "Can I get you a drink?"

He also doesn't seem accustomed to having guests. "Nah, I'm all set. Sit down with me, kk?"

Jazz grabs the remote and slides right over the arm of the opposite edge of the couch, and then drops down. Once sitting, he leans forward and sticks his chin in his hands. "Wanna watch a movie?"

I shrug, and then think of a better idea. "I'd rather talk, I think." I mirror his action by leaning forward and placing my chin in my hands, as well. I'm not about to simply bail out on all of the strategies on the list I've already put into play that have gotten me this far.

"Okay, yeah... that's cool. We'll talk." Jazz leans back and looks at me to see if I will copy him. I don't care what Emmy says—this guy knows what's up.

But not wanting to disappoint him, I lean back too.

"You helping to close up at Beans and Greens tomorrow, Chance?"

"Uh huh. I'm on cleaning duty. In the barn—all of the vegetable racks have my name on them."

"That's not too bad. I'm breaking down and winterizing a bunch of the farming equipment and I gotta pack away all of them outdoor carts into storage."

"You'll be doing heavier work than me." I conjure a mental image of his flexing biceps during hard labor and try not to drool.

"I'm cool with that."

We talk about work for the next hour until it hits me that I should leave while the conversation is still interesting. Leave him wanting more, right?

This is when I have to break out the big guns. First, I mentally review all of the flirting tactics I've mastered, and I start by presenting Jazz with a warm and gracious smile, because that's number one on The List.

"Why're you so happy?" He genuinely wants to know what is responsible for my sudden shit-eating grin.

"Well, to start with... I l-l-laaaaaaove pizza." I make the word love as suggestive as I dare. I can now check off the box in front of "be highly flirtatious." And then it's time for the "lingering soft touch." I reach out and place my pinky finger on his forearm. Odd, maybe, but it is certainly a very soft touch, and I leave it there for about fifteen seconds, which I think qualifies as lingering.

He studies my pinky like it's something green that's dripping out of a baby's nose, and then he blinks slowly a couple times, as if he believes that homemade cheese pizza sexually arouses me. Or maybe he's just plain not gay and my pinky is trespassing on forbidden territory.

Time to distract him. "And JoJo's a doll."

Jazz breaks into an honest grin that matches my sultry smile. "She's a good kid. I was kinda worried you wouldn't be into hangin' with her."

"No worries on that account, Jazz." I lick my lips hoping that it will inspire him to wonder what they taste like.

Jazz slides closer to me on the couch. This is going well—better than I'd hoped for, in fact. "You sure you gotta head out?"

I nod. I have to believe what the online article says—*my* absence will make *this* heart grow fonder. "I have to be at work by nine in the morning."

"Yeah. Me too." Jazz pulls himself to standing and offers me his hand. "Here, bro', I'll walk ya outside." I take his hand and he helps me up.

I'm not sure I'm too thrilled with being referred to as "bro", but *mmmmm... how gentlemanly.*

Maybe outside is where he'll kiss me. The muscles around my heart tighten.

For a minute, we stand there gazing into each other's eyes in the dark apartment. Then he shakes his head, as if to break out of his stupor, and says, "Come on."

I follow him downstairs and then we again stand quietly, both of us looking across the street at my car. "Well, I guess this is good night." So maybe it's a lame thing to say, but I have to fill the silence with *something.*

"Yup, I'd say you're right." *Awkward much?* "You drive the Volvo wagon?"

"It used to be my mom's and got handed down to me."

"Cool. Volvos are real dependable." *Car talk? Really?* Jazz takes a step in the *wrong* direction, as in, away from moi. "Well, maybe we can hang out again sometime?"

"Um, sure." I successfully resist the urge to step toward him, grab him, and plant a wet one on his lips. Not an easy urge to battle.

"So… uh… see yah."

And that's it. He sends me a wave that gets kinda cut off when he turns around, and then he walks toward his apartment building, never once glancing back.

Chapter 14
My Hero

I wake up late. That, in itself, is a minor dooza-palooza, to be sure. After reciting every curse word I know and a few of the ones Emmy has invented, because there's absolutely *no way* I'm going to be able to present Jazz with the best version of myself with ten minutes prep time, I gather the presence of mind to hop into the shower. At a minimum, I will rock clean and shiny, if somewhat flat, locks. And after I towel off, I douse my neck in *Utter Breath of Earth's Girly Silky Second Coming,* pull on a pair of acid-washed skinny jeans I find on the floor near my bed, and throw my last clean sweatshirt, the one that says, "Born this Gay," over my dripping wet head. And I'm out the door.

I don't even have a chance to log onto my computer to review The List for The Plan, leaving me with only a vague notion of ways to make Jazz fall head over heels in love with me swirling around in my brain.

Curses....

It's five minutes after nine when I get to Beans and Greens, and I will admit to glistening (sweating) slightly and being a tad out of breath as I hop from my car and start to run across the parking lot toward the barn.

"Look—the sissy's skipping!" It's Eddie the Appalling, creative with his insults, as always. "Bridezilla must be late for her wedding!"

I need a confrontation with him right now like I need a fourth hole in my right earlobe. "Bite me, piss-ant!" I shout in his direction.

Very predictably, he doesn't like my response one bit. "You talkin' to me?"

I stop, look very obviously all around me, and then fix my eyes squarely on his. "Hell to the yes. I don't see any other piss-ants in the vicinity. Do you?"

"I've about had it with you, faggot...." This retort is certainly less than creative.

"Look, Edwin," I decide to try to reason with him, although I realize that reasoning with pure testosterone in the human form will be a challenge. "Let's just pretend we never had this morning's little meeting. I'm late for work, and it looks like you are too. We should just get our rears in gear and get where we need to be."

Edwin clearly isn't enthralled with my idea. He steps closer and grabs me by the neck of my sweatshirt with one hand. "You're just beggin' to get your ass beat, know that?"

I will admit to experiencing an inkling of real fear. I may be on the tall side, but Edwin looks as if he got stuck on the evolutionary path in the region of "Neanderthal." He's big and brawny and hairy and his fists are the size of grapefruits. "Just let me go, Darling." I do my best to sound a cross between bitchy and bored, but I'm not sure I pull it off.

"Uh-uh, jag-off. Been waitin' to get you alone offa school grounds for way too fuckin' long." His other grapefruit fist joins the party at the neck of my sweatshirt, and I'm pushed hard against Jennifer Lourde's SUV. It crosses my mind that she wouldn't be pleased if the indent of my butt cheeks, or worse for me, my head, was imprinted forever in the passenger door of her shiny new vehicle. "And I figure last time you and me went at it under the bleachers, you just got lucky."

He holds me against the truck with one hand and draws the other fist back, and next thing I know, I'm lying on the ground gazing up at him, a bunch of bright white stars circling around his head. It occurs to me that one of my fabulous cheekbones might have just been smashed into smithereens.

I hold my breath and say a quick prayer to I'm-not-sure-who, hoping that Eddie the Appalling is satisfied with a brief show of violence, but naturally I'm not that lucky. He crouches down and draws his arm back to take another swing, so I cover my head, which seems like the only reasonable thing to do under the circumstances.

Oh, and I wait for the pain… which doesn't come.

When I lower my arms from my head, I see two bodies scuffling around on the dirt parking lot to my right, and then, like magic, Edwin is beside me on the ground, clutching his nose and making a howling sort of noise. I look up this time, and amidst the persistent white stars of my daze, I see the worried face of Jazz Donahue.

"Hey, Chance, you okay?" He reaches down to help me stand.

Resisting the urge to snark, "Do I *look* okay?" I grab his hand and struggle to my feet. I'm bombarded with conflicting emotions—relief, anger, fear, humiliation—and I seriously worry I might start crying. But then I remember a detail from The List. I mumble incoherently, "Number five."

Jazz's troubled expression demonstrates that he thinks I'm not right in the head. He clearly believes Edwin Darling knocked a couple of screws loose with his well-aimed punch. But he's wrong.

5. Let him be the hero.

Like I had much of a choice.

And despite my stunned state, more words from The List for the Plan pop into my brain, with a clarity I can't explain.

* **it's in every man's nature to want to be the strong protector**

Didn't the online article point out that whether he opens a jar of pickles for me using his brute strength, or if he defends my honor like a valiant knight, my man lives to perform such masculine tasks? Honest to fucker-nelly, I think it says that somewhere. Looks like I just provided Jazz with another stellar way to fall in love with yours truly.

Not that it doesn't hurt like a rabid fox dangling from my cheekbone by just his frothy fangs. Cuz it does.

I watch as Edwin rises shakily to his feet and staggers off toward God-only-knows-or-cares-where, whining, "I think you broke my nose, Donahue…."

I don't feel one iota bad for Eddie the Appalling or his stupid bloody nose—after all, he started today's bullshit—but I nonetheless toss a measly three points his way because his shenanigans have allowed me to check one more item off of The List for The Plan.

"This shit ain't finished, princess." I firmly believe that this line, grunted backward over Eddie's shoulder, is directed at me. "You're gonna pay for your wise mouth."

Again, I shudder.

And again, Jazz asks, "You doin' okay?"

"I think I'm all right. Could use a bag of ice." Jazz is still surrounded by a few too many bright white dots for my taste, but I'm almost certain I'm not going to nosedive to the ground in a dead faint.

For the love of RuPaul, you took one punch. You're fine, I tell myself.

"I'll go grab you some ice from the freezer in the barn." Jazz turns to leave. "You wait here."

As in, wait here alone? I think not!

"I'll come with you. And, um… let's just tell everybody I walked into something."

He looks at me with those sincere brown eyes. "Like a tree?"

"Sure, why not?" I smile at him wearily, and then I nod. "Like a tree."

Jazz grabs my arm and holds me close to his side as we walk, and I think that under any other circumstances, I'd be ecstatic.

Oh, who am I kidding? I'm in the arms of the guy I'm *so* crushing on!

This is everything!

Chapter 15
Please Not the Gender Thing

It must be about eleven at night when my parents sit Emmy and I down at the kitchen table, serve us Pad Thai from a take-out box, and ask us questions (interrogate us) about our college applications. I'm shocked that they make this effort—they must be curious about what their son is going to do with his future. Truth is, I haven't yet actually filled out college applications, as I'm not planning to apply anywhere Early Action or Early Decision, and so I have until the winter to get my applicational ass in gear.

My mother is tall, reed thin, and definitely shares my resemblance to Prince Harry of Wales, but in an aging female hipster way. A strange mental image, I admit. "Chance, have you decided which essay prompt you are going to respond to on The Common Application?"

I bite my thumb to stifle the urge to say, "as if you give a shit," knowing the sarcasm would be lost on my clueless 'rents.

Unfortunately, Emmy speaks up for me. Loud and clear, like always. "I keep telling him he should do the one about challenging a belief or an idea."

Tell me she's not going to say this…. Please, no—not the gender thing.

My father wears his gray hair in a long ponytail down his back. He likes to think of himself as cool and with-it, like an artsy, antique flower child, but I strongly suspect that he's really just one enormous ego. However, Emily has peaked his curiosity. "Why do you say that, Emily?"

She doesn't reply because she's still wrecked from the emotional backlash of the unwanted discussion of her Juilliard essay, which I have recently started to refer to as Juilliard-Em-mania. Side note: she's not going to stop suffering from Juilliard-Em-mania until her essay is written, edited, and submitted to said school.

When we get to my room later, she says, "I don't want to talk about my essay right now." She's as squirrelly about discussing that essay as I am talking about my gender identity. "It's a work in progress, that's all I'm gonna say." Ironically, she adds, "You really should write your Common App essay on being gender fluid. Or gender queer, or whatever it is that you are." She stares at me expectantly, as if waiting for me to explain in a single brief sentence the gender quandary that has plagued me all my life.

I gulp as we climb on my bed. This subject is totes off-limits, and I'm pretty sure Emmy's aware of this. I mean, how many times do I have to change the subject, shoot her snotty looks, or tell her to shut the bleep up, for her to get the freaking picture?

"You want me to yapper-halt, don't you?" Emmy tosses her new word out there without batting an eyelash.

Yapper= chat nonstop, and halt= stop. It doesn't take a rocket scientist to figure this one out.

"Yes, I want you to shut up about my so-called gender crisis! I'm a gay male. Case closed." There's this part of me that wants to open up to my best friend, to spill out my confusion and fears, and to get a heavy dose of much-needed advice. Instead I snap at her. Go figure.

"Why can't we just talk about it, Channy?" She snuggles closer to me so our bodies are aligned, and is soon propped up on one elbow, staring at my profile. "I'm your best friend, don't you trust me with your innermost thoughts and feelings... and secrets?"

Emily's bottom lip pokes out in the manner of the classic pout, and since she's already sniffling from our dinner conversation, it doesn't take much for the dam to break. Soon she's sobbing on the hot pink sleeve of my "The Other Team" baseball shirt.

The screaming maniac who is currently doing an excellent job of impersonating Chance César wails, "I'm not keeping anything from you, Emmy—I'm keeping it from me!"

"Wha-what do you m-mean?" She stares at me, a peculiar blend of shock, curiosity, and defensiveness in her expression, and suddenly all I can see is the awkward auburn-haired girl with long braids hanging down her back and a freckled nose stuck into a book, who I met at the bus stop one morning before school when she moved to town in the eighth grade. The person who changed my life by ending years of solitary confinement.

Time to make a big decision. Do I say, "It's simple, hunny. I don't so much want to *be* a girl as I, on occasion, *feel* like a girl?" Or maybe, "I'm *so* sorry that my lack of a clear gender identity makes you uncomfortable. You ought to try being me for a day."

Thankfully the slightly cooler and more collected Chance grabs the bullhorn out of raving Chance's hands and does his level best to spell out the closest thing to the truth. "It's like this, Em, I've *so* had it with people trying to label 'what' I am, but at the same time I'm even sicker of *not* having a label."

She looks supremely bewildered.

"I guess I'm sort of like your Juilliard essay—a work in progress."

Her expression still says "what the f?" so I try again. "I'm not hiding, really. I'm just not ready, willing, *or able,* which is most critical here, to define it. If I had my wish, there'd be no pressure for me to 'define' my gender, anyway." I form those strategic air quotes that I detest so much with my trembling fingers. "I'd just live my life in a gray zone—like I'd be as femme or masc as I feel at any given moment—and I'd stop asking myself endless questions about what I am." After an extended loud and very dramatic sigh, I add, "I'd just live."

That's a mouthful, and it's also the best explanation I can give.

Surprisingly, Emily nods just once. "I think I get it."

"You do?" Cuz I sure as shit don't.

"Yup." Her hands move to her braids as if without thought and she starts to unweave the hair, but her gaze is super glued to my face. "Doesn't it feel good to share, Channy? I know I feel better."

I nod, dumbfounded for the second time tonight. "And seriously, Channy, your attitude toward your fam—well, I'd classify it more as *poopatude*. Here's a strong suggestion for you—work on it."

"That's so random," I utter under my breath. This criticism of how I interact with my fam is out of the blue, but she's probably right. There's no use in being such a bitch when it comes to Mom and Dad. They're doing the best they can.

And although Emily wants to cuddle up to me, and chat about school and music and TV shows, I just can't get back on track with her tonight. I'm pissed cuz she forced me to show my gender-confused hand before I was ready, and after a half hour of stilted conversation, I tell her, "I'm beat, girlfriend. Time to yapper-halt and hit the hay."

Chapter 16
Little Miss Independent

Mom and Dad are long gone by the time we wake up, so we scramble a few eggs and wolf them down, and then we hit the local Java Joe Coffee Shop because we have serious shit to do. The ice built up in my heart in regard to Em's betrayal gradually thaws as we attack our homework, which we want to get out of the way. After that, Emily opens up her Juilliard essay—I can tell it's her college essay she's working on cuz she gets this glazed over, dreamy look in her eyes like she's lost in thought, and then every once in a while her brow furrows and she bursts into a fit of writing.

While she's doing that, I occupy myself with studying The List for The Plan. Out of the ten ways to make Jazz fall madly in love, I have now accomplished six of them. After a long and tedious inner debate, I decide that I will go with number three for my next strategy, which will be my seventh attempt at sealing the deal with Jazz.

3. Be Little Miss Independent—stay cool and focus on your own extremely busy life.

With the exception of Emmy, I'm a lone wolf. I never rely on anybody. Learned the stupidity of thinking my friends had my back the hard way. In grade school, there was a time when I tried really hard to hide the girl in me from the other kids. First of all, I didn't understand why I wanted to sketch fancy-looking bedroom sets with frilly comforters and lacy curtains at recess when the other boys wanted to run the bases, but I still got the picture that it was wrong. So I did my best to join them, and I faked genuine interest in sports. Being naturally athletic made this "passing for a real boy" much easier. But I loathed every second of it.

This one day when I was about nine, a friend, Shane Pederson, randomly stopped by our house, and Mom, unaware even back then of my need for her protection, sent him right up to my room, totes unannounced. He found me lounging on my bed atop a pink and white polka-dotted piece of jersey cotton that I'd sewn into a rather primitive duvet cover (what do you want—I was freaking nine years old!) and surrounded by a dozen sketchbooks, which were wide open to display my colorful designs of up-to-the-minute trendy boudoir décor. Shane took one look at me, framed in pink and white polka dots, designing flowery pastel bedspreads, and he was out of there. The next day at school, I was officially labeled "girl-boy" and I never again had another play date.

Long story short, I have become a very independent person.

* continue with your busy life in exactly the same way as before

Okay, that I can do. Uber pie-stroll.

* don't turn into one of those needy girls he's been with before

Well, that's not likely to happen without major surgery, but I get the gist. Don't be clingy. I can do this too.

* fall in love with yourself first—you can't love anyone else till you love YOU

So this part is the dooza-palooza. How am I supposed to fall in love with Chance César when I don't know *who he is?*

Then it hits me. *Fake it 'til I make it.* This I can do.

"What are you so caught up in, Channy? You look like you're about a zillion miles away from here?"

Emily's voice startles me.

"Earth to Channy... I asked you a question! *Hello!* What're you daydreaming about? Is it Jazz? *Hmmm?*"

"Hashtag, sorry, not sorry." I gather my thoughts. "I'm thinking about how difficult it will be for me to fall in love with myself."

"Um, first world problem, buddy."

Emily's right. "I'm looking at number three on The List for The Plan—the one that says for me to be Miss Independent. The article suggests that I have to love myself before I can love another."

At times, like right now, for example, Emily can be very abrupt. "Come on. Let's make like wagons and roll."

Huh? "You want to leave the coffee shop?"

I get one of those *duh* looks as Emmy packs up her crap. "We're going for a walk."

After stuffing all of my shit into my rainbow-striped messenger bag, we grab our coffees and head out onto the Main Street sidewalk.

"So, what did the article say to do?" she asks.

"It just suggested that by being Miss Independent, I'll make him go out of his mind with desire."

"So... you shouldn't be too clingy?"

"That's what it said."

"How you gonna do that?"

"I'm thinking that I'll just promise myself I won't change any plans I have with you so that I can go out with him."

Emmy smiles widely. "Good call."

***

I don't know why we go to the park cuz town parks often spell T.R.O.U.B.L.E. for kids like us. There are about ten cool kids from our high school hanging out near the picnic tables. They refuse to acknowledge us as we pass them, which compels Emily to do something totes obnoxious that will be sure to get their negative attention. So she breaks into song—the refrain from Alexa Rae Joel's "Notice Me"—that makes them glance over, throw us some major shade, and just as quickly, look away.

But there's always one bad apple in the bunch. "A fruit and his fruit fly! Wonderful!" he shouts. Emmy sings louder.

There's one thing that bothers me more than the aggressive behavior of Eddie the Appalling and his backwoods thugs, and that's the apathetic attitude of the rest of the student body. I'm convinced that their goal, by ignoring us, is to let us know we're less than zero, not worthy of a glance. And nobody can officially accuse them of being bullies, right? Technically, they've never lifted a finger or directed a cruel word at us.

It just pisses me off because these kids are, in my mind, bullies who don't bother to put in the effort to pick on us. They just sit there and pretend we don't exist and feel as if they're totes innocent of being cruel.

Well, newsflash, assholes—there's cruelty in silence.

"I've been thinking, Channy...." We're now seated beside each other on the swings at the far end of the park. "I think maybe the reason Jasper hasn't fallen for you is because you never fight."

"Are you suggesting I punch him?" Clawing him is more my style, but I say, "punch" for the sake of argument. I kick my bubble gum pink Chuck Taylors in the dust, fully aware I will be scrubbing out the dirt spots tonight.

Emily releases one of her indelicate guffaws into the fall breeze. "No, that is not what I mean, and yapper-halt with the poopatude."

I shrug. "My bad."

"I just think that maybe you shouldn't agree with him on every tiny detail." Her voice takes on a breathless quality and I know she's excited about this. "If you never challenge him he'll think you're a doormat."

Hmmm.... That possibility never crossed my mind.

"So when this concept hit me a couple of nights ago, I googled 'disagreeing with your man'. And my suspicions were confirmed." Emily gets off her swing, steps behind me, and takes hold of my swing. She inhales deeply, and pulls my swing back as far as possible. When she lets me go, she shouts, "And catch him off guard! It'll make him respect your opinions more!"

As I fly through the air, I decide that maybe she's on to something.

***

Later in the week, Jazz had called and invited Miss Independent out to the movies. Not really as his date, more as two buds taking in a flick together.

Um, Rome wasn't built in a day.

"Let me check my social schedule," I'd replied. "Because I *have* a life."

My not so off-the-cuff reply had been met with what I'd suspected was hurt/baffled cell phone silence.

"Hmmm... let's see. Friday night... Well, good thing you didn't ask for Saturday—big plans with Emily." A bold-faced lie. "Or Sunday... cuz I... I'm busy... busy doing... um, another kinda A-list thingy... on... uh... Sunday." The second half of my tall tale had tripped me up.

There had been more silence.

"Well, lucky for you, I'm free." I'd sounded like a Class A douche bag, so I'd added, "I'm looking forward to it," hoping that would take out a portion of the sting.

***

It's Friday and I'm at the movie theater and... and Jazz is not.

When Madonna starts singing "Express Yourself", I scramble for my cell phone and, lo and behold, it's The Target on the line.

"Um... Chance?"

Who else would be answering my phone? "Hashtag have I been stood up?"

"Well, no. Somethin' like, came up."

"Cut to the chase, Donahue."

He hesitates, but only briefly, and then spills. "I have to watch my sister again tonight... and we need to go to Walmart to get a birthday present for her friend and then I have to take her to the Roller Palace for a birthday party... and see, my mom thought she had the night off... but a co-worker called in sick. And so, this sucks but, while JoJo is roller-skating, I told Mom I'd grocery shop because she has to work all weekend and...."

Jazz is a hot mess. "And you can't make it to the movies?"

"Like... like, no." I can actually hear him swallow. "Sorry, dude."

"Care for company tonight?"

I swear he gasps. "Doing errands and stuff?"

"Sure, why not?" *Remind him you have a life without him.* "Well, I cleared my extremely busy social calendar to go to the movies with you, so I'm free."

"Sorry 'bout that." *Shit.* If he were a puppy his tail would be tucked between his legs.

"No prob. We'll make it fun." Who am I kidding? I'd prefer to drive around town doing errands with Jazz than sit silently beside him in a movie theater. "Where should we meet up?"

"How 'bout the Roller Palace in like thirty minutes. I'm already at Walmart, so we'll run in and get the gift, and then I'll drive her there. You can dump your car and we can go shopping together in my car. 'Kay?"

"Sounds like a plan to me."

Doing errands together—this is like relationship realness.

***

Jazz is leaning against the passenger side of his car, waiting for me as I pull into the Roller Palace parking lot. He looks delicious in today's crisper-than-usual white T-shirt and loose Levis. And his shoulders in that denim jacket—they totes slay me! After I pinch myself to make sure I'm not dreaming, I get out of my car and stroll over to him as if I have all day. It's a challenge, I will admit, not to fling myself into his arms.

"Hey, Chance. I'm wicked sorry 'bout the whole movie thing." I watch his eyes as they read the one-liner on my sweatshirt. *Yep... your gaydar is accurate.* His lips move as he reads. When he's finished reading, he doesn't make any kind of a facial expression at all. Not a snarl, not a smirk, not a frown, nor a smile. It's like *blank city,* as if he has no idea what *gaydar* is.

Is that even possible?

"Bonjour, Jazz." His eyes lift enough to meet my gaze. "Don't think anything of it."

"Thanks... I guess that's what friends are for." My heart sinks at his reply. To add insult to injury, he adds, "If you are ever in a pinch, I'll be your most dependable buddy, too. No worries on that account." *Now* he smiles.

I throw him the stink eye and push him aside. Jazz opens his car door with a curious tilt of his head, and I get in.

Before he closes the door, he looks at me very directly and says, "Ya see, my mom works a whole lot. And in the winter when I'm not contributing cash because my job is over with 'til spring, she grabs any extra hours she can get."

I keep all of the money I earn at work in the summer for cash to spend during the school year. And if I run out of money, my 'rents just leave more for me underneath the coffee maker, or one of the other small kitchen appliances. But Jazz actually subsidizes his family's living expenses. This is eye-opening info, *fo sho*. "So you must help out more with JoJo during the school year?"

"Yeah." He closes the passenger door, trots around the car, and then climbs in. "That's why I gave up sports after school. I used to play football, basketball, and baseball, but in high school practices got too long and there are lots of games on weekends, you know, so...." His voice trails off.

I think maybe I melt a little. "Y-yes, I know." What else can I say? He'd had to give up more than just his social life to help his family. He'd given up about everything. "So where do you shop for food?"

Pulling out of the parking lot, he says, "Usually at the Market Basket. It's cheapest."

***

At the Market Basket, Jazz shows me a bunch of big foil bags he took from the backseat of his car. "I brought along these freezer bags so the cold stuff won't melt while we wait for JoJo."

"Good thinking." I grab a carriage and start pushing like I'm the one in charge. "So how about we just go up and down the aisles in order?"

"Sure. But there are a bunch of aisles I don't need anything from so we can skip them." We start in fruits and vegetables.

Jazz examines each potato with the scrutiny of a county fair vegetable judge. He actually weighs the apples to see how much he is spending. I don't think my mother has ever used one of those scales. She just grabs what she wants, bags it up, and leaves.

Conversation between Jazz and I unfolds peacefully as we stroll through the soup and pasta aisles. The meat department is where I decide to make things interesting. "Don't get Ball Park Franks, Jazz."

He turns toward me, hot dogs in hand. "Why not? They don't cost too much and JoJo likes 'em."

"Well, did you know that Kroger Simple Truth Uncured Beef Hot Dogs are made from animals that are raised humanely? No antibiotics or hormones, either. You really should be thinking of JoJo's health." I'm not sure why I remember these facts, but I know I acquired them doing a science research project during freshman year on the constitution of hot dogs, which had led to way too many "Chance loves wieners" jokes. But I'm not going to miss this opportunity for us to experience a minor disagreement, so, as Emily informed me, he'll respect my opinions more.

"But JoJo likes Ball Parks...." Despite the mild challenge, he has returned the package of Ball Park Franks to the refrigerated bin, indicating that I'm winning this debate. Score five points for Chance César. I'm officially *not* a doormat.

"Simple Truth Hot Dogs have no preservatives, MSG, or gluten either," I augment my argument with these indisputable facts. "Not to mention that the animals are vegetarian-fed." If this isn't "an intellectual challenge to his usual way of thinking" I don't know what is.

Jazz steps over to the Simple Truth Hot Dogs and picks up a package. "You sure got strong feelings 'bout hot dogs."

I blush. Jazz's remark reminds me of what the boys in my ninth grade science class had asserted—"Chance César is a wiener man"—but I know that his intention is not cruel like theirs had been.

"Well, seein' as these Truthful Hot Dogs cost more, I just won't get JoJo her Oreos. She can live without 'em for a week."

Who feels like shit now?

I'm the guy who is basically stealing cookies from the mouth of a little girl. I snatch the Simple Truth Hot Dogs from Jazz's hand and replace them with the Ball Park Franks. "The thing is, as long as you don't eat them every day, no brand of hot dogs will really hurt you too much." I'm not sure whether or not that is true, but it sounds good. "Now let's go get JoJo her Oreos."

***

The best part of our non-date comes after we pick up JoJo from her roller-skating birthday party. A girl named Lily—I swear it's the very same girl who had her eye on my Miss Harvest Moon tiara on the night of the pumpkin festival—is going to sleep over at Jazz and JoJo's house, so I treat them all to frozen yogurt at The Brain Freeze Yogurt Shoppe. By this point, I have totes given up my effort to disagree with Jazz so that he knows I'm not a doormat, because I sort of suspect that Jazz never thought I was a doormat to begin with.

The girls sit across from us in a booth by the front of the shop and we all eat Honey Jalapeno Pickle frozen yogurt, which sounds disgusting but is awesome in that sweet-and-salty-at-the-same-time way. JoJo and Lily color in the picture of frolicking cows on the menu with the yogurt shop's broken crayons, and Jazz and I play hangman on napkins.

Afterwards, he drops me off at The Roller Palace, and actually gets out of his car and walks me to my Volvo—like we are on a real date! I unlock it with my remote and he opens the door for me. I'm grinning like an idiot at this point.

I so badly want a kiss but I'm totes aware there's no chance in hell of that happening, mainly cuz we've never acknowledged that we're on an actual date, and secondarily because two little girls are staring at us from the backseat of his car. I mean, their noses are pressed against the steamed up glass. So he winks and I wink and we say good night. And I get on with my extremely busy (not so much, but Jazz doesn't need to know this) life.

Chapter 17
You Only Live Once

"Hey, Chance… it's me." I'm not expecting a call from Jazz. In fact, I just saw him in the hall right after school let out, and he was on his way to retake a Chem test he messed up on.

"Hi Jazz. What's up?"

I've never before heard Jazz sounding stressed, because along with being the Pumpkin Carving King, he's also the king of the laid back attitude. Today is different. "Can ya do me a favor? I really need help."

"Sure thing. What can I do you for?" I try to be funny but it falls flat. He doesn't even giggle.

I hear a long sigh and then, "JoJo isn't feeling good and needs to get picked up early from school. But if I leave school now I got to keep a D on my Chem test."

"You want *me* to pick her up and take her home? I don't think the school will let me take her."

"I'll have my mother call and give permission. It's just—I gotta do this test and Mom'll get in trouble if she leaves work."

I don't hesitate. "Of course I'll get her. The Doubleday School?"

"Yeah… she'll be at the Nurse's Office."

"Done. Now go retake your test."

***

Yolo (my newly made up name for JoJo—I have my reasons) and I sit next to each other on the worn couch in their living room, waiting for her mom or brother to come home. She really is sick—I can feel the heat of her body cuz she's leaning up against my arm. And she isn't saying too much, which is further evidence of serious illness. I flick on the TV.

"What do you want to watch, Yolo?"

The girl shrugs and I know she must be feeling like shit squared. All kids care about what they watch on TV.

When the door opens, a woman enters carrying a couple of grocery bags and her coat folded over her arms. She looks completely disheveled, but I can still see the resemblance between her children and her. "JoJo, baby… Mommy's home." Mrs. Donahue rushes to JoJo and looks at her with a tender expression I can't remember ever seeing on my own mother's face. "Tell me, sweetheart, where do you hurt?"

As Jazz's mother places her hands on Yolo's face, she shakes her head. Yolo mumbles, "My throat… and my head. Got a headache so bad, Mommy."

After shaking her head one more time, the woman says, "Hello, dear. You must be Jasper's friend, Chance. I'm Mrs. Donahue, Jasper and JoJo's mother." The woman looks at me with a guilty expression, like she committed a serious sin.

"That's right. I'm Chance César. It's very nice to meet you." I'm used to people giving me a strange look when they hear my full name, and Mrs. Donahue doesn't disappoint. But within a second she's again fully focused on her daughter.

"Thank you so much for picking up Jo from school. You really saved us." Mrs. Donahue pushes her shoulder length brown hair back off her face. Although she's talking to me, she's looking at Yolo. "Did you give her any Tylenol?"

I shake my head. "I thought it would be better to let you do that when you got home."

"Well, then, will you sit with her while I get her Tylenol and a glass of water, and a pillow and blankets?"

"Sure—not a prob."

By the time she comes back with everything Yolo needs, Jazz is stepping through the door. "Hey, Jo… you okay?"

She moans a sort of "uh-uh" sound as her mother makes her comfortable on the couch and gives her medicine. I can see the love and concern in both Jazz and Mrs. Donahue's faces as they bend down to check on her. Seeing that, I'm not joking, I start to tear up. This scene is freaking touching.

"Before you say no, Mom, I'm tellin' you that I'm gonna stay home from school and look after her tomorrow. So no worries."

This is a lot to take in.

"You already missed school to stay with her last week, and as a result you almost failed your chemistry test. No, I'll take the day off work."

They are looking at each other as if they're going to argue about who is going to sacrifice more, and that's when I realize it. This is a real family. Tired, broken, poor—yes, yes, and yes. But their interactions possess the important ingredient mine is missing: they actually love each other.

"I guess you guys don't need me here anymore. I… I'm gonna take off."

Mrs. Donahue sits down beside Yolo on the couch. "Thank you so much, Chance. You really helped us."

"I'll walk you to your car, dude." Jazz grabs my coat and leads me to the door. We head down the stairs and out to the street.

"I hope Yolo feels better soon."

"Yolo?" He looks at me with confusion, but I'm used to that by now.

"You know the expression 'you only live once'? I call her Yolo now, cuz Yolo is the kind of kid who goes for what she wants. She has the YOLO attitude."

Jazz shrugs, and then nods his agreement. "Well, you saved *Yolo's* butt. And mine and my mom's, as well. You really are a great friend."

Just what I was hoping for—to be Jazz's bosom buddy. I do my best to smile but what I offer him is no Miss Harvest Moon grin, that's for dang sure.

"We'll talk soon, yeah?" Jazz asks, but before I have a chance to say, "yeah" in return, he's gone.

Chapter 18
The Manipulative Method

It's like the line goes dead on our relationship.

Not only does Jazz not call me for the rest of the week, but he also doesn't show up at school. I figure he's taking care of his sister. And I seriously hope Yolo isn't too sick, but still, it only would have taken him five minutes to call me.

So, yeah, I'm hurt. And I'm pissed off. He told me he knew he could depend on me. In fact, he'd done just that. But when the going got tough, Jazz basically pulled a Houdini act.

***

Emmy and I sit down in the front of the cafeteria to eat our usual garden salad, drizzled with today's special dressing, a surprisingly delightful raspberry vinaigrette. The front of the cafeteria translates to "the safe zone" for weird kids, as teachers tend to congregate near main entrances.

"Looks like you're going to have to go about this the devious way, Channy." Emmy states this as if it's a simple matter of fact. "And speaking of which, there's a certain number on the list that you've been avoiding. I think the time has come for the deed to be done."

"What freaking deed?" I need to better control my poopatude.

She ignores my outburst. "Yes, ma'am." I don't mind when Emmy refers to me as a female, but she's the only one who's allowed to do it. "Don't tell me you forgot the devious details."

It's not that I'd forgotten about all things dastardly, but I've been avoiding putting number eight into practice. Jazz, however, has left me no choice. And in a flash, Emily has placed her laptop on the lunch table and we're staring at number eight.

8. Use the manipulative method.

"I had hoped it wouldn't come to this, Emmy."

"If you want to trap The Target, this step is mandatorbs."

I don't say anything in regard to her use of the word mandatorbs, because I'm almost certain it isn't the word of the day. Especially since she stole this word from yours truly.

"Shall we examine the details?" she asks.

"Let's, shall we?" Yes, an Emily expression.

* give attention, withdraw attention, give attention, withdraw attention—repeat until he's yours

"So you treat him like a yo-yo, basically." Emmy's voice is a shade too matter-of-fact for my personal comfort.

"It seems kinda… well, kinda mean, don't you think?"

"Desperate times call for desperate measures." Emmy is totes on task, and there is no playfulness in her demeanor. Nor are there any sexy mouth movements, for the record. "Make a date, break a date. He'll try harder to get you to the next time. Apologize and reschedule. Then do it again."

I stand up, assume the position (one hand placed on jutted-out hip, the other pointing directly in Emily's face), and protest, "I'm not doing that." There are limits—*I have limits.*

"Sit down, Channy. I get what you're saying, and if you can't handle the heat, then you're either gonna have to get out of the kitchen, or we're gonna have to take it down a notch."

Who is this hardliner sitting across the table from me? I stare at her.

"The next level down goes like this: you show up to spend time with him. You flirt with him. You laugh, you smile, you touch him—you know, you give. And then boom! You stop. Just like that. Cold as ice. That's the withdraw part, see?"

"I don't know. I'm a lover, not a—"

"You are a fighter, Chance." Emmy flicks an olive at me. "And don't tell me you're not. You fight every minute you are at this school just to get through the day in one piece!"

"So you're saying I have to fight for Jazz's love?"

"That's exactly what I'm saying! According to the online article, three rounds of this torture and he'll be eating out of the palm of your hand." Her voice is growing quite shrill.

"Calm down, girlfriend. I'll do it."

"There's more." She turns her laptop around to face me. "I want you to read this part out loud." She points to the screen.

* use reverse psychology

"It says to use reverse psychology." I'm not sure I'm into this part. "So?"

"Keep going,"

"'Warn him not to fall for you. This will activate his desire to chase you down and keep you for his own. In short, he will be compelled to fall in love with you.'"

"Next time he calls to see you, Channy, I want you to give, withdraw, give, withdraw. Three times."

"How's your essay going?" I venture.

"We are discussing *you* at the moment!" Her answer is clipped, suggesting the onset of Juilliard-Em-mania.

And I think: *Not well, her Juilliard essay is apparently not progressing well at all.*

"I'm willing to help you with your essay any day of the week, Em."

"Eat your salad." She snarls.

***

After school on Friday I receive a call from The Target. He explains that his sister had strep throat and he'd had a few very difficult days. But she's better now, and he wants to get together and hang out at his house.

Give.

"That sounds like fabulousness personified. I'd totes love to come over!"

Give.

On my way to Jazz's apartment, I stop at The Brain Freeze Frozen Yogurt Shoppe and pick up a quart of Black Licorice frozen yogurt. It's creepy looking, all inky black, and it has a strong licorice scent, but I figure that Yolo will think it's strange and new and fun.

And just a tiny bit more giving.

When I arrive at Jazz's house, he's waiting for me by the outside door. I park, runway strut right up to him and shake his hand, not letting go of it immediately.

Inside, I divide up the Black Licorice frozen yogurt into three bowls.

"Thanks for bringin' the frozen yogurt, Chance. Black licorice is my most favoritest candy, you know," Yolo tells me, so thankful.

"I had a feeling about that."

Jazz is ultra-stoked just to see his sister this pumped up. *Cha-ching!*

It's too bad I have to bring him down to earth. "You missed a lot of school this week, Jazz."

His smile falls and he nods. "I emailed my teachers and explained. It should be all right, I think. I'll try an' get caught up." Then he shrugs and makes a joke. "We look like three aliens. The Creatures with the Black Tongues."

Yolo and I laugh.

As Yolo finishes her yogurt, Jazz says, "Jo was pretty sick last week. I had to sleep on her floor for two nights so I could keep an eye on her."

I hang on his every word.

And I smile till my cheeks (and eyes) hurt.

Then Jazz puts Yolo to bed.

Withdraw.

When Jazz comes out of Yolo's bedroom, he sits down close beside me on the couch. "JoJo had to brush her teeth for like ten minutes to get the black outta her mouth."

"That's nice." I stare at the TV that just so happens to be off.

"I think she'll be okay to go to Sunday school this Sunday morning. But she was wicked sick, y' know."

"You don't say."

His breathing changes. It gets faster and uneven—he's growing nervous. "Um… everything all right, Chance? Ya seem kinda like, *different* all of a sudden."

Time to give again.

I turn to him. "No, no… really, hun, everything's fine. So did anybody bring you your homework assignments? Cuz if you'd called me, I would have."

"I almost called you, but every time I picked up my cell phone, Jo started whining."

I place my hand on his knee. "Don't worry about it. I just figured Yolo was very sick and needed all of your attention." As if I'd actually been that mature about the days that had passed by without a phone call.

And withdraw.

I lift my hand from his leg.

This process is strangely reminiscent of hair care… Rinse, wash, repeat. Give, withdraw, and repeat.

By the third round of this "emo-cycling", I'm mentally fatigued, and Jazz looks like he's been through a war. Beyond that, he won't look at me at all and is barely saying a word. That's when it hits me—the guy *has* been through a rough week—a sick sister, sleeping on the floor, missing school. And now dealing with moi.

So I decide against employing the tactic of reverse psychology. I nix my plan to warn him not to fall in love with moi. No more head games for to-night—they're exhausting for both of us. "Do you have any board games?"

We spend the rest of the evening having a blast playing Apples to Apples.

Chapter 19
Love Spell

It's time to regroup.

In some ways, it seems like I'm not getting anywhere with Jazz and I blame this epic failure largely on my inability to pick a gender and embrace it. I mean, it *must* be the reason that none of the scientifically proven strategies have made Jazzy-boy fall deeply in love with me. Like, what else could it be?

Tonight my silky robe isn't feeling as sweet as usual against my skin and it's definitely not doing its job of evoking a relaxation response. So I drag myself out of bed, grab the remote control off the top of my bureau, and then turn on my television, confident that anything that's on in the middle of the night will bore me into the soundest of slumbers.

As I switch the channels I decide that late night television has been taken over by the Gods of the Infomercial.

Just great....

But also boring, and isn't that the point?

So I hop back in bed, turn on my side, close my eyes, and listen.

"Lonely? Seeking love? Look no further. I am the renowned Beverly Hills Psychic, Marcus Vistabliss, and I can help you get the emotional commitment you deserve. I have twenty-five years of experience uniting needy souls who are seeking one another, but just can't find their way together. My internal senses are finely tuned into the world around me… and because of that, I am your answer. Your heart does not have to accept the emptiness any longer—it does not have to keep on hurting. So don't waste your time on love spells that don't work. If you are ready to break down all of the barriers to love in your life, call me at…."

Love spells.

That's it.

A love spell.

I will cast or do or perform—not sure of the correct lingo in this situation—a powerful love spell on Jasper Donahue. And he will be helpless to the magic, and then putty in my hands. He will fall in love with the fabulous moi, despite my ambivalence toward gender… um… gender commitment.

But the online research in regard to my *ahhh-mazing* idea will have to go down tomorrow. Having discovered the way to finally get a firm hold on Jazz's heart, I suddenly feel incredibly relaxed. And ready to sleep.

As I drift off, my overworking brain slows down. But it doesn't come to a complete halt—I mean, this *is* Chance César's mind we're talking about. So my thoughts go where they always go when I'm trying not to think of anything at all—gender issues. I consider a point my mother brought up just last year. She said that when I was small, like six or seven, or maybe younger, I used to insist I was a girl. Mom didn't tell me this information with a wrinkled up nose and a heavy dose of vitriol, like she was pissed off or wigged out or in any way disgusted by it—instead, she told me with a shrug and a yawn. It was as if her son having lived as a princess in his own mind since before he was in preschool had no effect on her, whatsoever.

Images of grade-school moi—scuffing around the house in Mom's pumps and guiltily sneaking into her bathroom to sample the lipstick and perfume—creep into my sleepy mind. And how I'd wanted one of those Bratz Dolls—with its glorious oversized head and slinky body and inter-changeable smexy shoes—with every fiber of my being. I would have given my right arm for Cloe. Platinum blonde hair and light blue eyes—I think I wanted to *be* that fantabulous doll as much as I wanted to have her for my own. In fact, as a young boy, I had a whole string of Bratz-sharing girl BFFs who now won't so much as say hi as we pass each other in the hallways at school.

Because I'm a freak.

Yeah... a freak, she-he, fairy-boy, circus sideshow, Bozo the Clown... and the list goes on.

Before I have a chance to mull over the rest of the names I've been called so routinely at school—and also at work, and at the mall, and at the park—I flip onto my other side, and let sleep claim me (I like the way that sounds).

***

To include Emmy or not to include Emmy, that is the question.

The instructions on the website do not specify as to whether I need to be alone to conduct the spell. And Emmy has been instrumental in carrying out The List for The Plan to this point. It seems cruel to cut her out at what could be the critical moment.

I press B for *Bestie* on my cell phone. Before she has a chance to say hello, I'm in gear. "Emmy. You busy today?"

I can tell from all of the pathetic whimpering sounds that I woke her up. "Nah... I put the finishing touches... (adorbs squeaky yawn) on my Juilliard essay last night. Gonna send it in this morning."

"You happy with how it came out, BFF?"

There's a brief silence while she's pondering my question. And her voice is brighter when she comes back with, "Yes, I really like it. My parents read it and said it was fucker-nelly awesome, and I am now fret-liberato."

Fret-liberato… hmmm. "Worry free? You are worry free?"

"I am *relieved.* And here's a confession to start the day: I wrote about you."

I gasp dramatically, which isn't newsworthy. "*Moi*? You wrote your Juilliard essay about Chance César?"

"Uh huh."

"How did you manage to incorporate *me* into your college essay?" I am genuinely curious, and at the same time anxiously hopeful that Emmy didn't make a mega-huge (fatal) error.

"Well, the essay question asked about why I wanted to be an actor and my personal goals. But it also said that we could write about our lives and how our art is connected to the world… and our passion for people."

I wait, still unsure as to how I fit into this essay topic.

"You, Channy, are the person who showed me it's okay to let it all go and to just be me, the *awesomesauce* individual I am. On the stage and in real life—because, in case you aren't aware, all the world's a stage."

Yeah, yeah… the world's a stage. Cut to the chase, girlfriend. "How did I do that?"

"You always let your true self show even when it's hard—when it gets you ridiculed, or punched in the face. And at the end of the day, everybody at school might think you're a complete freak, but they respect the heck out of you."

"Thank you, I think." It seems I have succeeded in doing something important, although I'm not exactly sure what.

"Channy, you define the expression 'march to the beat of your own drummer' and because of you I just don't give a hoot what the peanut gallery thinks about me."

Tears rush to my eyes cuz I am floored by the impact I've unknowingly had on my best friend's life. "Con-drag-ulations on finishing it."

"Well, thanks. I started the essay with a descriptive image of you strutting the runway as Miss Harvest Moon. And I think my statement about freedom of expression that I put in at the very end really frosts the cake!" Now that all traces of sleepiness are gone from her voice, the jubilant state of her fret-liberato rings out clear as a bell, but "frosts the cake"? That one is new.

Emily, however, is psyched, so… *Smi-zee!!* I break into a grin.

"I'm giving you life, right?" She recites an expression I probs use too often.

"Yaaasss! This is everything!" (Another expression I may possibly over-use.)

"Okay, so what's on your mind this morning, Channy?"

Her question brings me right back to reality. I swallow a gulp of air. "I'm thinking of taking a detour."

"Wha'?"

"A detour from The List for The Plan."

"Oh. Do you think that's wise?"

I nod, momentarily forgetting she can't see me. "I only have two items left on The List that I haven't done and they're totes lame ones—something about being a decent friend and being yourself. Like *those* would actually make a dude fall for moi."

"So where is this detour gonna take you, girl?"

"Hopefully it'll take me straight into the arms of Jazz. Here's the deal: I'm gonna cast a love spell on him."

I hear a sharp intake of breath. "A love spell, you say?"

"Yup-ster."

"I have one question for you."

"Uh huh?"

"Why didn't you do this a week earlier?" Her voice conveys mega-annoyance. "The image of Chance César holding a wand, casting a love spell, would have fit perfectly into my Juilliard essay."

I laugh, but she's already laughing louder than me.

"Count me in, Channy. Can you come get me?"

"Of course, and we're gonna need to stop at the store to pick up a few items that are mandatorbs for the love spell. I have a list."

Her breathing is loud and fast. She utters just one word, "Hurry."

***

"The website says that Halloween is the perfect time to conjure a spell because the veil between the physical world and the magical world is paper thin," I explain.

"And tomorrow is Halloween, so we should be in like Flynn, right?"

I wonder who "Flynn" is as I drop the various shopping bags on the bathroom floor. Emmy and I had to trek around town to three different stores to get all the necessary materials for today's endeavor. "Yeah, I think this is gonna werk like a charm."

"Okay, you start cleaning the bathtub, Chance, and I'll cover the mirror and the window with the pink material we bought."

"Try not to rip the fabric cuz I'm gonna use it to make a bedspread and throw pillows after we cast the spell," I remind her.

Emmy hangs layers of pink fabric, covering the window and the big mirror with oversize rainbow-colored pushpins, and I use antibacterial wipes to clean out the tub. "You've gotta clean the whole bathroom, you know." Emily the drill sergeant pulls the paper with the printed instructions out of her back pocket and waves it in my face. "It says so right here."

"Kk. Why don't you go find my Speedo while I finish cleaning—it's in the top left drawer of my dresser."

She goes in search of my swimsuit, which I have prudently decided to wear, seeing as I do not want to cast the love spell in my full naked glory in Emmy's presence. *So* not cool. I finish wiping down the bathroom and then fill the tub with hot water.

"Stick this on—I'll turn around." Emily presses my tiny red Speedo into my hand and I quickly strip off my clothes and pull it up my legs. As I tie the drawstring, she informs me, "I brought the sea salt, too."

Feeling quite naked despite my swimsuit, I kneel beside the tub, open the box of sea salt, and pour a handful into my palm.

Emily sits on the closed toilet, watches and waits, her eyes wide. "Okay, go ahead and say it."

I nod. "All negative thoughts are washed away." I glance at the instruction sheet on Emily's lap where the words of the spell are highlighted in neon lime green. "Um... I am clean as of today."

"Now throw salt in the water."

Tossing half of the handful in, I continue with the spell. "Lots of souls will look my way, I will pick who I want to stay." I throw the rest of the salt into the steaming water, trying to do it with an exaggerated flourish of my arm, as it seems like the right thing to do in this situation.

"Think really hard about Jasper." She runs from the bathroom, calling behind her, "I'll get the candles and your IPhone. You picked a song, right?"

"Yeah. I've been listening to a lot of Christina Aguilera lately." I call after her, picking up the printed instructions she left behind, and glancing at the directions. "And the paper says that if you want to cast a spell on a soul mate, listen to music that's calm and peaceful. I think 'Genie in a Bottle' fits this occasion." *Like a freaking glove.*

"I have to agree with you there, girl."

I climb into the tub, and at first the heat is shocking, but after a couple of seconds I sink down slowly into the warmth. It feels good. The room is bathed in an odd, dull, rosy glow from the daylight shining through the thin pink material that now covers the window. Emily returns to the bathroom and goes back to work, putting the Christina song on and then lighting three white votive candles that she placed beside the sink. Almost instantly, the bathroom smells like Easter morning, as there was a sale today on Marsh-mallow Chicks Scented Candles at Job Lots.

"Okay, Channy. You need to close your eyes and relax."

Easier said than done, because taking a bath in the presence of... well, of *anyone*... is not the norm for me. But Emmy starts speaking in this hypnotic monotone voice, which is honestly quite strange, but also effective. My shoulders slump down as the stress exits my body.

"Focus on your body and how sexy and attractive you are."

"Smexy." I correct her and try not to smile, but I know I'm blushing. From head to toe, literally.

"Now think about the things you like about yourself." She leans down and murmurs into my ear, "I can help you here if you get stuck."

"No, I've got this—totes pie-stroll." *My style, my dry wit, my biting sarcasm, my ginger-hued good looks, my lean lanky frame, my....* Looks like I could go on all day.

"Shit on a shingle! I forgot to turn out the lights!"

Okaaaayyyy, Emmy's expletive *does* break the mood to some extent, but I'm able to find my way back to la-la land without too much difficulty.

"Here comes the critical part: Focus. On. The. Target." She says each word slowly and deliberately. And since I'm nothing if not obedient (ha!), I concentrate as hard as I can.

Amidst the dreamy music and the sugary fragrance and the raspberry shade of darkness, an image of Jazz forms in my mind. He's smiling, and it's that sweet guileless grin I've come to adore. I smile, too, cuz all of the small details, including the softness of his gaze and the perfect chestnut color of his hair, are just right in my mind's eye.

And then what feels like a plastic bottle nudges my shoulder. "It says you have to cleanse yourself thoroughly. Do you want to shave your face? Or your legs?" Emily giggles. "Or anywhere else?"

I shake my head, having shaved myself smooth as a baby's ass in the shower this morning.

"Well, scrub-a-dub, Channy, and then you need to repeat the lines you said before. But this time you have to add stuff about love—no worries, I'll coach you through it—and don't forget to think about Jasper the entire time."

"Can I open my eyes?"

"Nah, for safety's sake I'd keep 'em closed."

So with my eyes tightly sealed, I shampoo and rinse my hair, and then swish water under my pits. I figure that should take care of the cleansing part. All of a sudden, a firm hand is clutching the top of my head and pushing me downward. It crosses my mind, as my nose sinks below the surface of the water, that Emily is attempting to drown me, but common sense soon prevails, as she has no motive. And I recall that the online article had said I needed to be completely submerged, if only just once.

"Now say it—say the chant-thingy!" This is what I hear when my head pops back above the water. "Do it now so you don't screw it all up!"

At this point, I rub the water out of my eyes and open them. "Lots of souls will look my way, I will pick who I want to stay."

"Add this—I love myself, I am loving, and I am love!"

"I love myself, I am loving, and I am love!" Momentarily, I forget I'm in a tiny bathroom, and my voice rings out, brave and true, as if I need to fill an entire auditorium with sound. *Love is everything!! Yaaasss!!!*

"Shout it again to be on the safe side. And louder this time."

"I love myself, I am loving, and I am love!" My mother, who is downstairs making grilled ham and cheese sandwiches for Dad's lunch, must be totes confused at the sound of my impassioned declaration.

And just like that the lights are on and the plug drain is lifted.

"Out!" Emily is frantic. "Get out of the tub! You heard me—move it!"

I stand up and shiver, suddenly more aware than ever of the skimpiness of my tomato-red Speedo. *Do I actually wear this thing at a public beach?* But before I have a chance to rethink my beach attire, she grabs my arm and pulls me from the tub.

"Okay, before your bath I wrote your name in red on this paper and I wrote his name under it." She frowns. "I hope it doesn't screw everything up that I wrote Jazz instead of Jasper."

I shrug. "What do I do next?"

"Draw a circle around both names." Emmy sticks a red marker in my dripping hand and then takes the bag of cotton balls out of a shopping bag. She then rips open the bag and hands me the cotton balls, along with a container of honey from my kitchen. "Now drop the marker and dab honey on the circle with these cotton balls, but not too much of it."

I do as she instructs but the honey pools up in places.

"Here, time for the cinnamon. Lucky thing it has one of those sprinkler tops, huh?"

I do not respond other than to take the cinnamon powder from her and look at my partner-in-witchcraft expectantly.

"Repeat after me: With this cinnamon sprinkled about, my love spell is done. It will surely bring me love from my heart's only one."

Obediently, I repeat her words. Then a thought occurs to me. "I don't need a magic wand, or anything, right?"

Emily smirks. "Keep your wand in your Speedo, where it belongs." Then she dishes out the criticism. "You didn't say your lines with much expression at all."

I roll my eyes. "Keep going, Em—I'm freezing my ass off, pretty much literally."

"Sprinkle cinnamon inside the circle only." She can be very strict when she wants. And right now her voice is that of an Army drill sergeant merged with Little Miss Bossy. And before I know it, she shoulders me aside and fully takes control. Standing behind her, I watch as she folds the sticky paper in half and in half again. "Now, you need to carry this in your back pocket. At all times, mister! If it starts to dry up, go ahead and dab more honey on there. It *must* stay moist."

Fighting shivers, I take it from her hand.

"Love spell—a done deal!" Emmy's voice is harsh and shrill and I expect her to hoot, but she doesn't. Instead, she says, "We need to let the candles burn out by themselves, or the whole spell will have been a complete and total waste of time, which would be a dooza-palooza, because I don't have time today to do this whole damned thing all over again."

***

Back in my bedroom—dry now, but still dressed in nothing but my skimpy red Speedo—Emily is a bundle of questions. "So, do you feel different than before?"

"Like 'different' how?"

"Like, do you feel a stronger emotional bond with The Target? Are you tingling—and if your body is tingling, exactly *which body parts* tingle the most?" Her gaze is focused squarely between my legs. I drop my hands to preserve what little remains of my dignity.

I would like nothing better than to inform my BFF that certain body parts are tingling, but all I feel is cold and damp and very, very clean. "No tingling, Em. Not... um... anywhere."

Emmy shakes her head; her disappointment is palpable.

"So you really think my relationship with Jazz is gonna start now?"

"We did everything by the book, so it should."

I press the damp folded paper to my chest. "I can't say I'm feeling the love yet."

"Patience is a virtue." She grabs her coat off my desk. "Now get your clothes on, girlfriend. As much as I'm appreciating the view," she eye-balls my goose-pimpled flesh, "I can't sit around here all day with you half-naked—I gotta bolt! Like now! Mountains of American Lit to read."

"Kkkk." I grab my clothes and head for the marshmallow-raspberry bathroom to get dressed so I can drive her home.

***

Despite my name being, essentially, "chances are", I'm not one to leave much to chance. And I'll admit that I planned this *second* love spell in advance. I purchased vanilla oil and a red votive candle at Walmart, and thankfully, Emmy hadn't questioned me about them, but then again she'd been busy stocking up on Peanut M&M's, which is our fave snack. Unfortunately, before I began Love Spell #2, I had to break a tiny ceramic ladybug off of a refrigerator magnet to get another necessary material. And for this backup spell, I've chosen to use my *I Can't Even Think Straight* sweatshirt, because its deep auburn color brings out the highlights in my orange hair as well as the strands of reddish-gold in my eyes.

I pull out the printed instructions, read, and then carefully follow directions. First, I rub vanilla oil into the candle and the magnet. Next I put a drop on my "chosen garment"—my ICETS sweatshirt. I light the red candle, close my eyes, and imagine myself as the most smexy and desirable gay teen in northern New Hampshire, which quite possibly is true. As I'm picturing my utter irresistibility, I take the magnet and wrap it up in my sweatshirt. Three times I circle this magical bundle clockwise around the red candle, all the while keeping a detailed image of Jazz's earnest face in my mind.

"Lust magnet, lust magnet, lust magnet," I whisper breathlessly, per the website's explicit directions.

Three times is a charm, or so people say.

Tomorrow, when I strut my stuff wearing my *I Can't Even Think Straight* sweatshirt at school, Jazz Donahue won't know what hit him. Or why he is drawn to Chance César as if by an invisible force.

***

Everything has to be perfect today. So before I leave for school, I open my laptop, pull up The List for The Plan, and complete a mental checklist to reinforce the power of my love spells.

1. Smile well and often.

My teeth are clean—I resolve to save my plastic bag of gummy bears for after I see Jazz.

2. Men fall in love with what they see. Show him the best version of yourself.

Red lips-check
Pink cheeks- check
Guyliner- uh huh, and plenty of it
Mascara- you better believe it
Rockin' hair- spiked up, and ready for action
Signature scent- oh, yeah

3. Be Little Miss Independent—stay cool and focus on your own extremely busy life.

This one didn't work so well for me the first time around. Number three will take a backseat today.

4. Leave him wanting more. Yada, yada, yada...

Off to the backseat with you, number four!!

5. Let him be the hero.

I'll drop my pencil and let Jazz pick it up for me. A slice of pie.

6. Be a little mysterious—you are different from the rest.

I can rest assured that I'll be the only boy in full makeup and wearing a hoaxed sweatshirt at Fiske High School today.

7. Try flirting—yes, tease him mercilessly.

Oh, I will. I will... and it will be a pleasure.

8. Use the manipulative method.

Epic fail the first time I tried it. I banish you, number eight, to the backseat!

9. Friendship is key.

I already have a friend, thank you very much. Her name is Emily, and my hands are more than full with her. Number nine, jump straight to the backseat without passing GO.

10. Always be yourself—this is the most important of all.

Can you say Lamesville?

I slip on my *I Can't Even Think Straight* sweatshirt, slide the folded up, honey-dabbed paper into the back pocket of my worn light blue boyfriend jeans, and head for the door.

***

Chance César never sweats publicly, with the fine exception of today. I reach up under my sweatshirt and T-shirt to touch my right armpit, just to be sure I applied my Lady Speedstick this morning. It's significantly slimy under there so I know I have been officially deodorized. But right now I wish someone had invented facial antiperspirant—I'd be all over that, or at a minimum it'd be all over my forehead. As I enter the cafeteria, my forehead is sweating so profusely that I'm certain my eye makeup is running down my face. I must look like a horror show (The Rocky Horror Picture Show with non-waterproof mascara, to be precise).

But, as usual, I see The Target, sitting with his two clueless side kicks, and so I stop a couple of tables away, just to see if he is drawn to me in a manner that seems in any way magical. *Sha-blam!* His head turns to look at the cafeteria entrance and he sees me hovering fifteen feet away—I'm confident that the love spell (spells) is (are) working its (their) magic.

"Hey, Chance!" He waves at me without any restraint, whatsoever. *Has he ever before flagged me down with such gusto? I think not.* "Come here… got this cool thing me and JoJo made ya!"

Jazz is clearly unaware of all the staring eyes. Because if he looked around at the other kids in the caf, he would see that he is causing quite a spectacle, and he would tone his exuberance down, I'm sure. I mean, it doesn't take much to read everybody's thoughts: "Look-it—the faggot has a boyfriend, and he's a dumbass from the tech school."

Tessa smiles up at me sweetly. "Sit down, Chance. Jasper has been waiting for you."

I can't miss that Kyle smiles at me too, which makes no sense because his *friends* are supposed to keep the innocent Jasper from my evil homosexual clutches. I plant my ass beside Jazz.

"JoJo got so much candy trick-or-treating last night that she went and decorated this bag for you and then filled it up with every kind of candy she had doubles and triples of. Plus she don't go for Skittles, so you got all of them."

I look at the table and there's a brown paper bag that has been carefully

95

decorated with markers, so it looks like a cat. A very Carrot Top-looking cat, I must say. Complete with eyeliner and wild, bright red hair.

Jazz adds, "Jo is kinda nuts 'bout ya, Chance." I want to ask Jazz if Yolo's older brother shares her sentiments, but I don't have the balls. Well, I do *have* them, but I don't always want them.

"I don't know what to say. Tell her thank you… and I love it." If that completely ordinary response doesn't fly in the face of being "different from all of the other girls" I don't know what does.

According to my decision to reinforce the love spells with items from The List, I break into a wide smile, and then slip easily into flirtation mode. This involves my pinky lingering softly on his arm, my fertile red lips making seductive O-shapes (technique courtesy of Emily), several passes of my perfumed wrist by his nose.

"Oh, dear! I dropped my Chapstick!" I declare, tossing the small tube casually to the floor by Jazz's feet.

"Lemme get if for ya." It's almost as if Jazz has read the script for this occasion.

My hero! I don't say it, but I *do* bat my lashes.

"Um… Chance… I was thinkin' maybe we could hang out again this weekend. Say, maybe, Friday night?" He's staring at my lips as he speaks, no doubt mesmerized by their lush and fertile redness. "Prob'ly gonna have JoJo again, but, y' know, we had kinda a blast last time, right?" He looks at me quizzically.

The love spell werked! OMG—the freaking love spell werked!

"Yaaasss!" Oh, that wasn't even slightly calm and collected. "I mean, that seems doable."

Jazz smiles the baddest smile I've seen yet. "Awesome. Later in the week we can set up the details. 'Kay?"

"Kkkk." *Duh! Who the hell says kkkk?*

I stand up to head back to the library, my work here now complete. But I have a need to prove a point to myself, so I turn away from Jazz and wiggle my backside alluringly, and then spin around with the speed of light to see if I can catch him staring. And when I spin back around—lo, and behold—Jazz Donohue's eyes are glued to my ass.

The lust magnet spell is clearly a winner too!

"See something you like back there, big guy?" I ask in the most seductive of tones.

"Um… I see something kinda wet-looking."

Wet-looking? This is an unexpected reply. "Oh?"

"Dude, something ya got in your back pocket is leaking right through your jeans." He reaches behind me and pokes at my pocket with a single finger. "It's sticky… kinda feels like.…" He places his finger directly on his tongue. "Dude, hate to break it to ya, but you got honey on your butt."

I turn back toward the doorway and laugh a little bit too loud, and a lot too fake. "Gotta go, Jazzy. Catch you tomorrow!"

Chapter 20
Abandon Mint

I feel confident that the love spells have worked on Jazz. After all, on Monday at lunch, he couldn't flag me down obviously enough, and he couldn't ask me to his house fast enough. He came bearing a gift, which he *said* was from his sister, but that's a mere technicality. A gift is a gift, right? And I'm certainly not one to look a gift horse in the mouth. Even if his lips are totes captivating.

Sitting in The Brain Freeze Frozen Yogurt Shoppe, waiting for my after-school meeting with Emmy, I lick at a boulder-sized scoop of Abandon Mint frozen yogurt off the top a chocolate-dipped waffle cone. Not my favorite flavor, but it serves me right because I didn't wait for Emmy to arrive to place my order.

My phone beeps and I pull it out of the front compartment of my backpack, fully expecting it to be Emmy with a lame explanation of why she's late. But the text is from Jazz.

Chance-
Super sorry for this, dude, but I gotta bail on Friday night. Talk soon.
Jasper

Well, shit. Not only did I get dumped, but Jazz offered no explanation, and there was absolutely no groveling either. Maybe the love spells have *not* worked as well as I thought. The pure shock of this thought makes me drop my frozen yogurt cone onto the floor.

"Hey, butterfingers!" Emmy comes just in time to see my mess-up. She leans down, grabs the cone, and tosses it into the trashcan. "You okay?"

"He blew me off."

"*Who* did *what* to you?" She makes a sexy lip gesture and waggles her eyebrows.

"It's nothing like *that*." I know that Emily is oh-so-wrongly focusing on the "blew me" part of my statement. "Jazz just texted me and canceled Friday night."

She looks stunned. "But we did that love spell by the book."

"Yeah, I know. And I don't know what to make of this. We must have missed something."

"We can do another love spell tonight. I'm not as loaded down with homework as usual." She stops to think. "There was that other one we decided not to do—the one where it said we had to start stomping and clapping and then, in time, chant 'Love me or die. Love me or die.' We could always try it. I'm game for pretty much anything."

Yes, there is that one. "We decided against it for a reason, though, remember?" I had pointed out to Emmy that threats of violence should be only employed as an absolute last resort.

"So is it back to The List?"

I reach behind me and touch the damp honey spot on my backside and then lick my finger. I am uber fed up with coming home from school every day with a sticky left ass cheek. "Yeah… I think I'll go over The List for The Plan tonight with a fine-tooth comb. See if I missed anything subtle."

"The Target should be totes in love with you by now, according to the specifications of the online article along with the additional insurance of a love spell."

Two love spells, I think. "Maybe he's highly resistant to suggestion of any kind."

Emmy sends me an I-seriously-doubt-that glance and I know she's thinking of Jazz's seeming lack of sophistication.

"Stop throwing me shade, girlfriend, and, in any case, there's no real rush. It doesn't look like I'll be seeing him this weekend." I glance at the bright green spot on the floor that my fallen Abandon Mint frozen yogurt left behind. "I'm gonna require another scoop of Abandon Mint yogurt so I can fully enjoy my pity party."

"Come on, Channy. Let's head to the counter. This scoop's on me."

***

Not to say that I kept my phone basically right beneath my chin for the next four days, but I kept my phone basically right beneath my chin for the next four days. Yes, I was oh-so-pathetically waiting for his call, which I am aware fully explains the need for the phrase "get a life." But Jazz hadn't been at school on the Thursday or Friday after he had called and cancelled our playdate, and now it's Sunday night, and I still haven't heard from him. And although I'm frustrated that all of my elaborate plans to make him fall head over heels in love with me have apparently tanked, I'm also growing genuinely concerned.

That's when my cell phone, which I placed on my chest before I lay down on my now "love-spell-pink" wrapped mattress, starts singing Express Yourself.

"Yo." I don't check the number. It's Emmy—who else would it be?

"Hi, Chance." The deep voice is so not Emmy's.

Yaaassss!!! This is what ninety-nine percent of my insides shout. One percent says quietly, "It's about frigging time you called, asshole."

But my voice is calm. "Jasper," I say blandly. In my opinion, he hasn't earned the right to be called Jazz any longer.

"Um, sorry, no. It's Jazz."

I try not to roll my eyes even though I know he won't see, but it's an epic fail. "Whatever."

"I'm sorry I haven't been in touch for a couple days. My mom's been real sick. I was lookin' after her, gettin' her to the doctor, goin' to the pharmacy, bringing JoJo back and forth to school, and stuff."

Oh.

"Mom caught JoJo's strep throat and had to go to the ER because she couldn't even swallow." He stops talking for a second and then clears his voice. "Alls she could do was spit into a rag whenever she needed to swallow."

Well, that's definitely TMI, but I get the fucker-nelly revolting picture. "I'm sorry."

"Not your fault, dude."

And then there's silence.

"Gonna take JoJo to the library after school tomorrow. But first I gotta stop by the cable company and pay up or we're gonna lose our TV and internet at home. They already warned us like twice."

"Want me to pick up Yolo at school and take her to the library?" I'm *so* freaking pissed off at him. *Why am I offering to save his ass again?*

"That's cool of you to offer, but there's a bus she can take to the library from her school. Could ya be waiting for her at the library, in case I get held up?"

"Of course." *I'm a Class A sucker.*

"You're such a cool pal." *Ugh—so not what I'm going for.*

"Thanks."

"I'm not gonna be at lunch tomorrow seein' as I'll probably be collecting my makeup work. So, I'll see ya at the library. 'Kay?"

I don't say kkkk cuz it's not even slightly cool. "Sure. The libes after school, it is."

"Thank you, bro," Jazz offers.

One more silence, and then I say, "Later."

I have research to do.

It's midnight, and despite a slow-burning anger at Jazz that is singeing the edges of my consciousness (oh-so-dramatic), I'm still busy jotting down my plans for tomorrow at the libes on neon-colored notecards. I've sifted through every detail of the now notorious online article and have uncovered some hidden gems I missed the first five hundred times I read it. "You, dah-ling, need your beauty sleep," I tell myself firmly, and so I wrap it up by copying down a suggestion from the article onto a neon pink notecard, of course.

Everybody goes wild over a fun-loving girl! Get wild and crazy and he'll go wild and be crazy for you!

Chapter 21
So-o-o Not in the Mood

I can only hope that things go better in the library than they did in the crowded hallway right after school. Eddie the Appalling's apparent obsession with seeing yours truly break down into a torrential downpour of sobs seems to have rekindled itself while I was busy fixating on my nonexistent love life. This afternoon, he refused to let me enter the boy's room by the back exit, accusing me of not meeting the criteria for its use. Edwin and his tribe of hoodlums, arms folded across their burly chests, blocked the entrance when I tried to get in.

"Girls' bathroom is over there, she-he!" Edwin spat, pointing across the hall. That remark hit just a tad too close to home cuz honestly now and then I feel like an imposter when I do my thing in the boys' restroom.

So I ignored him and tried to squeeze between several tree trunk bodies.

"Wanna make somethin' of it, princess?" That was about when my arch nemesis grabbed me by the neck of my sweatshirt and stared hatefully into my eyes.

And because I was meeting Yolo at the libes, I really didn't want to make a big deal of this. So I wriggled from his grasp, spun around and walked away. But as Darling spewed his hateful verbal venom my way, I couldn't resist calling back over my shoulder, "Listen up, everybody! A baboon is speaking!"

Yup. My ass is grass. A half dozen burly oafs will probs be waiting for me in the parking lot tomorrow morning, ready and willing to make me regret my very birth.

Will I never learn to keep my freaking mouth closed?

***

Jazz stares at my bright yellow sweatshirt that has a cartoon drawing of Jesus on it, and says, *OMG. I said I hated FIGS.* And judging by the look on his face, I have done my job in being totes unpredictable with my wardrobe choice. But maybe more so unpredictable in the *horrified* way, as he keeps looking at his sister to see if she has caught on to the little "funny" scrawled across my chest. I pull off my sweatshirt and underneath I wear a plain white T-shirt, just like he does. *Sigh.* I have never much liked level playing fields.

At least I won't have a wet spot on the back of my skinny jeans to fur-

ther appall him, I think. It hit me on Friday that I could put the honey-cin-namon-love-spell paper into a Ziploc bag before slipping it into my back pocket, in order to keep my ass dry. Maybe the love spell is failing, but the Ziploc bag is working like a charm.

"Come on over here, Jasper," Yolo says as she grabs my hand, and so I grab Jazz's, and, like a human chain, we walk to our table in the back corner of the library.

"Looks like you guys already got to work, huh?" Jazz looks down on the table at the open books about horses strewn all about.

"Chance is helping me with my project on wild horses." She looks up at me like I rescued her kitten from a high tree branch. "He's real smart, Jasper."

Jasper blushes. I melt. "Yeah, I kinda figured that out already."

"Well, let's sit down and study," I suggest lamely. Not a fun suggestion. Not even slightly unpredictable. If I had a ruler I'd give myself a couple of quick lashes on the wrist for being so dang boring. I'm not going to get *anywhere* with Jazz acting all ho-hum like this. In fact, "Men love women who make them laugh," is a direct quotation from the article.

"JoJo, you okay if me and Chance sit down and talk for a second?"

She nods happily. "Oh, yeah… Chance showed me how to use the printer and bought me a printer card. I'm gonna print pictures from these books." She hoists a tall stack of hardcovers into her skinny arms. "Might take me a while."

"We'll come and check on you in a few minutes," her ever-responsible older bro says.

"I'm a *big* girl, Jasper. I can do it by myself." And Yolo lifts her chin with the attitude of this year's Miss Harvest Moon, turns, and stalks off toward the printer.

"Thanks, man. You saved my butt again. What can I do to make it up to ya?" He looks at me squarely, his eyebrows raised, and just for a second I wonder if he's flirting. But then reality sets in. He's never flirted before, why should today be any different?

"You can tell me what IDK stands for."

We both sit down. Jazz tilts his head with confusion, and replies, "Um… I don't know?"

I mirror his head tilt for bonus points, and come back with, "I don't know either—*it seems that nobody does!*"

Jazz looks at me strangely, and shrugs.

Yes, Jazz… that was what we call a joke.

He just lifts his backpack from the floor and drops it onto the table.

So far, so bad....

I try again. "There's something I've been wondering for a long time now."

He continues to look at me in a guarded way.

Nonetheless, I press on. "What do you call a magic dog? Do you have any idea?"

Slowly, and almost cautiously, he shakes his head.

"A labracadabrador." I laugh, hoping like hell that Jazz will follow suit. He doesn't.

"Did my sister teach you those jokes when you were showing her how to use the printer?"

If he were anyone else, I would think he was being mean. But this is Jazz, and he's *never* mean. I don't think he knows *how* to be mean. He is clearly not susceptible to my fine-tuned wit. So I move on to being silly, as it is alleged in the online article, to be one of the most satisfying aspects of a relationship.

I turn toward him and lift my fists like a boxer. "Watch out Mr. Dona-hue—cuz when people don't like my jokes I get awfully angry." I take a couple of playful swings at his solid bicep. And then I make a frisky jab at his chin.

Jazz grabs my fist as it makes its way toward to his face, and he's fast—like one of those Venus flytrap plants. "I never said I don't like your jokes." He drops my hand.

"Jeez, don't have a hissy fit… I was just fooling around." This is the first time *I* have actually spoken those words to another human being.

"Guess maybe I'm not in the foolin' around kinda mood." Jazz replies, still not smiling.

"So I suppose you don't want to make goofy faces and take selfies to-gether?"

Jazz shakes his head. "Not so much."

"Or play mouth-catch with this bag of popcorn?" I pull a snack-size bag of Smart Food out of my backpack. I'd made a special trip to the Ready Mart before school to pick it up for just this purpose.

What he says next makes the blood freeze in my veins. "Why're ya always playin' with my head, Chance?"

I don't think he's expecting an answer, so I don't offer one.

"I'm up a creek, dude! Behind on schoolwork and probably not gonna graduate on time. An' my mom's got no more sick days 'til next year, and Jo is always comin' down with stuff."

""B-but Jazz—"

"Can't you ever be serious? Huh? It's all a big game to you, ain't it? My feelings for ya and my whole life—it's all nothin' but a game to you!"

I'm fairly certain at this point he's not going to want me to tickle him mercilessly in a circle around his belly button—my next preplanned tactic—which might get him to laugh, but it certainly wouldn't score any points for moi. So I don't mention it.

My midnight planning—all for naught! What a complete waste of neon notecards. But what's far worse than my obvious personal failure in my effort to make him fall for me is the look on his face. Jazz's expression is a miserable combo of pissed off and depressed. Like I stepped on his pet goldfish and then flushed it.

"No, Jazz. It's not like that at all…." Tears of intense emotion rush to my eyes, but I sniff hard and manage to keep them inside.

"Dude, what I really need so bad right now is a friend. Somebody I can talk to—like straight-up honest. Y' know?" He stands up and starts collecting Yolo's books and placing them in a pile. "I don't think you know how to be somebody's *real* friend, César. Cuz in the end, it's all about you."

Ouch. Like a knife to the gut.

And although he's pissed, Jazz's eyes are clear when he searches my face for the truth, which I have not exactly been giving him lately (ever). He lifts his backpack and Yolo's schoolbag, throws them over his shoulder, stalks to the copy machine, grabs Yolo gently by the wrist, and leads her from the libes.

"I want to be your friend." I don't stop long enough to plan my words—they just fly out of my mouth. "Let me be your friend." At this moment I don't care if Jazz is gay or straight, or whether we're destined to be friends or lovers. He needs a friend as much as I do.

But he can't hear me.

Cuz Jazz is gone.

On my way out of the library I stop in the men's room and toss the Ziploc bag stuffed deep in my back pocket into the trashcan.

Chapter 22
LGBPTTQQIIAA+ *Aaaaahhhhhh!!!*

"You're giving up?"

"I'm choosing *not* to look at it that way, hun," I reply, in a futile effort to be patient.

"Never thought I'd see the day that Chance César would throw in the towel. I'm… I'm stupi-boggled."

"Well, don't be." I rarely, if ever, ignore the introduction of a brand-new, Emmy-invented vocabulary word into my life. But this is one of those rare moments. "Things have changed."

"Changed? After all of the effort we put into The List and The Plan and the love spell?"

I turn my phone off speaker and lift it to my ear. "Look, girlfriend—Jazz's life ain't no pie-stroll." I speak with a sassy tone. "I've screwed up with him big time." This is not a detour from the plan. It's a bailout.

"And your life is a pie-stroll?"

I know what's coming. "Don't go there," I warn her using my deepest, most growly, voice.

"Let's put it bluntly, shall we? You can't decide whether you wanna be a boy or a girl! That makes for a rough ride through life, cowboy!" She sucks in a deep breath, and I know she has plenty more to add, but all she says is, "Admit it, Channy."

Not to be a totes drama queen, but I end the call without saying goodbye. And honestly, at times like this I wish wholeheartedly that I had an old-fashioned telephone I could slam down onto its receiver with indignant fury. Pressing the "end call" button is just so anticlimactic.

I flop back on my bed and lie there spread-eagled, suddenly resigned to the fact that my life is in ruins. I have only one option left: I'm gonna hold my own private pity party. I reach for the box of Cheez-its on my bedside table to enhance the experience. And slowly but surely I start feeding myself the cracker-tranquilizers. As I decompress I try to sort it all out.

Starting with the obvious BIG ONE, in terms of my problems.

Why does Emily have to throw my undeclared gender status in my face? It seems like the very minute she has an opportunity, she drags my personal shit out into the open, where I don't want it. Can't she see I just don't want to go there yet?

Although I'm mad as hell, I still must fight the instinct to call her back and say, "I love you, hunny. Excuse my emo self and tell me you love me back." Emily *is* the only one who is there for me, and maybe she's right. I'm in complete denial about how major a problem my gender confusion is, and that can't be healthy.

But I have other problems than this, no doubt, as recently my life has so very abruptly and completely gone to hell in a handbasket.

*** I pissed off Edwin in a big way, so school should be a totes danger zone.

*** I tried to manipulate Jazz just one time too many, and he's had it with me.

*** I'm pissed off at my only friend in the world and I'm fairly certain the feeling is mutual.

*** And let's face it, my parents are no prizes and it's way too late for me to register them for Parenting 101.

What to do… what to do….

This part is actually easy to figure out. I'm just going to put first things first and conduct online research.

Hello, Google. You and me are gonna werk it hard!

I close the box of Cheez-its, get up from my bed, and relocate to the desk where my laptop is already open.

This is not the first time I've performed an online search of this nature. When I was a couple years younger, my searches went like this: "Help! I don't feel like a boy or a girl!" More recent searches have included such topics as gender identity, gender confusion, gender spectrum, and gender expression. And there are times I research more specific terms—just trying to find my box. The place where I fit in. Unfortunately, I must report that I haven't had too much success in achieving this goal.

When I press LGBT this comes up as an instant choice in my browser: LGBPTTQQIIAA+ *Jeez'*. There are so freaking many terms to describe people whose physical body doesn't match his or her sexuality and gender identity. There's *androgyny* and *bigender* and *cross-dressing.* Add to the mix *gender fluid, queer, genderqueer, third gender*, and *transgender.* And so many more. I've already studied them, one by one, with the scrutiny of a defense lawyer in a capital punishment case. And none of the labels fits like a glove.

I close my eyes for a second and try to picture myself showing up at the high school's guidance office and saying, "Hello, Mr. Boothby. My problem today is that I can't figure out if I'm a boy or a girl. Can you help me with this?" Mr. Boothby would be shocked. He'd blush and stutter and probs end up requiring mouth-to-mouth resuscitation. *Ewww*….

So instead, here I am propped up against the brand-new puffy pastel plaid pillows on my bed, trying to find a label for Chance César's gender identity. I turn to Old Faithful: The Comprehensive List of LGBTQ Terms and Their (perplexing) Definitions. All the terms and meanings are set up in this long list and… and it's kinda like a menu.

"To start things off, waiter, I think I'd like an extra-large order of *androgyny.* For a main course, I'll go with the *queer,* I hear it's simply amazing, but please hold the *cisgender.* I'll need a side of *cross-dressing,* and how about a grande *genderfluid* to drink? For dessert, just hit me with a big bowl of *bigender.*"

Am I supposed to pick just one label? If so, how do I decide? So many labels fit, but just as many don't. And of the ones that fit, none fit perfectly.

Emily's right. I don't know if I want to be a girl or a boy or something else entirely—like a unique combination of boy and girl that I don't have to determine until I wake up in the morning. And that I can easily change at the drop of a hat. In short, I am an official hot mess in the gender department. And despite the warzone that is my brain, I'm falling asleep, which does nothing to prevent the oh-so-predictable questions. They file in slowly and sluggishly, however, as I'm close to la-la-land.

Why is it so hard for me to pick a side—boy or girl—and just be that? Yes, this first question is marked with a distinct "woe is me" tone.

Why should I have to wear clothes that make me feel like a complete fake? And why can't I identify as a guy who just so happens to like to look pretty on occasion, and maybe feel feminine more than just every now and then? And does wanting this stuff make me a freak? Question for the ages.

Do I want to change, and become a girl? I'm thinking that for the most part I'm cool with what's hanging between my legs, not that boobs wouldn't be cool fashion accessories.

Will I ever be accepted just the way I am? By friends? By other guys? Will Jazz accept me? These questions cannot be answered right now, so I'm forced to toss them into the "shit to worry about at a later date" basket.

And finally I ask myself the only acceptance question that *should* really matter. *Will I ever be able to accept that I don't fit neatly into any gender box I've come across?*

I pull my ultrasoft, lemon chiffon, eight-hundred thread count sheets up over my face and close my eyes, thinking of how I'm gonna be goofier with Emmy so she'll forget how I hung up the phone on her, and look more attractive so Jazz won't care that I was manipulative, and be even snarkier so the thugs won't dare to harass me.

I'll fix things tomorrow.

Chapter 23
Friendship is Key

I wake up with three things on my mind—the first of which is Emily. I need to fix things with my bestie before school. So I pull the oldest trick in the book.

I pick up my phone and press B, and when I hear Emmy's voice I mumble something incoherent.

"Did you just say you're beguiled by me?" she asks, clearly annoyed.

"No. I said I must have butt dialed you." I snicker so she knows I'm messing around. "But since you're on the phone with me now, um…."

The line goes dead, though, and I grimace because being hung up on almost physically hurts. I *so* deserved that.

#epicfail

***

Next on my fix-it list is what I screwed up with Jazz. But I can't repair that until I see him at school, which means I'm first going to have to deal with Edwin Darling and his backwoods thugs, which is number three on my more than slightly scary to-do list. *Ugh.*

***

As I predicted, the thugs are waiting for me in the parking lot. Lucky for me, though, Vice Principal Lowen is out in the back of the school supervising (patrolling), and he was a linebacker in college, so I'm confident he'll be able to keep me safe.

I know that I need to make Eddie the Appalling's gang think twice about bullying me, but all I have available to use as a weapon is my sharp and biting wit. As I pass by them, they predictably mutter stuff like, "Homo, faggot, she-he" and all I say in response is, "In order for you to insult me, I'd have to value your opinion."

Needless to say, the thugs just look confused in the face of my response, as they only understand obvious insults. But when Edwin notices that Mr. Lowen is focusing on two cars that seem to be fighting for the same parking spot, he grabs me, pulls me right against him, and says, "You gotta learn to shut that smart trap o' yours, ya ugly orange-haired troll." Now *that's* a new one.

To this I respond with my best Southern twang, "It's a cryin' shame that stupidity ain't painful."

Unfortunately, my down-home voice rings out into the cool morning, attracting the vice principal's attention, and he yells, "Darling, let him go! And César, get over here!"

As I walk away from the group of grumbling assholes, I can't resist tossing out one more zinger. "Oh, poor boys… did Hello Kitty say goodbye to you?"

"*Now,* Chance—get your butt over here *now!*"

I saunter away, careful not to appear intimidated, which is key to my survival. When I arrive at Mr. Lowen's side, I look at him expectantly, waiting for my lecture.

But all he says is, "You never learn, Chance. Haters are always going to hate and fighters are always going to fight." He shakes his head at me in disappointment. "All they have in their lives is anger. You have so much more. So don't antagonize them—rise above them and they won't bother you."

Although I feel as if he just recited the lyrics of a sappy Taylor Swift song, something about the look in his eyes makes me think that he might just have a point. "Thanks for that tidbit of advice, Mr. Lowen." I say it without sarcasm, which surprises both of us. And I think I'm going to give what he suggested a try.

I head for the school building.

I step into the cafeteria hesitantly, the movement in complete opposition to my typical runway strutting. Do I saunter to my fave water fountain for a quick sip? Um, no. I just lean against the wall in the front of the caf, and do this freaky stalkerish thing.

Jazz notices me staring at him after about five minutes. I expect him to get up and sit down on the other side of the table so he's not forced to look at me anymore, but he doesn't.

Jazz stands up and walks to where I stand. "Hey, Chance."

Hope is renewed in my heart! In other words, yay.

He clears his throat and by the look of concentration on his face, I know he's gonna say something important. "Dude, I want to say sorry for blowin' up on ya at the library." His dark eyes finally meet mine. "That was real wrong."

I open my mouth to speak, but he presses on my lips with his finger so I'll stay quiet.

"I shoulda been more honest with ya. I shoulda just said plain and simple that I don't think it's gonna work out with us two as… like boyfriends. Even though I fell for ya real hard."

He's in love with me! Yaaasss!

He's dumping me! Noooo!

"I think you're lookin' for a dude who's way more complicated than me, Chance. And though I want you for my own, I don't think I can make ya happy."

I sigh. Then I kick myself. Mentally, that is.

"You're real smart, to start things off. And you're so pretty and super sexy and ya smell like heaven, I swear. Plus ya got a real busy life goin' on with tons of cool stuff to do… And I don't think you've got a single care in the world. It's like you're always smiling and funny and surprising and—"

"No…." It is all I can think of to say.

"Yes, Chance." He continues, "It's just not like that for me. I gotta take care of my house and my sister all the time, and sometimes… sometimes it's real hard for me. But it's what I gotta do. So I can't act goofy and funny all the time 'cause I got so much on my mind. You need to be with a person who's not real simple, but who's bright and shiny and awesome and… and that person ain't me no matter how much I wish it."

I succeeded in my plan. I made Jazz Donahue fall in love with me.

He fell in love with my captivating smile and my Cherry Chapstick lips and my sweet scent. I made him think I was mysterious and at the same time the life of the party—he even believed that I had far better things to do than spend time with him. He truly thought I wanted to leave when I really so badly wanted to stay.

I did it. I made him fall in love with me.

WTG, Chance. Way to go….

"So, I was hoping that us two could be friends, 'cause, dude, I really am into hangin' out with you. Somethin' about the way we can just loosen up and talk to each other, super open… and I don't want to lose that, Chance." The way he's looking at me is so freaking sincere.

And I don't want to lose it either. But I know that in winning the game of love I almost lost it all.

"I'd like to be friends, too, Jazz." My voice is weak and shaky. I can't stand to look at him any longer. And I can't smile or flirt or do anything at all except try not to cry. "Um… I gotta head out. But call me, kkkk?"

I think he nods, but I don't stick around to be sure. I can only hold back the tears 'til I make it through the lunchroom door into the hallway.

#epicfail2

I don't fare much better in my real lunch block. Emily just plain old doesn't show up. When I sneak a peek in the library, I see her there, her nose buried in a book. Just like the day I met her.

#epicfail3

I suffer through the rest of the day feeling empty and lonely and regret-ful. I avoid tears, except in Classic Lit class when we discuss *Wuthering Heights,* and then I totes lose it. Nobody in the class is particularly shocked by my tears. I completely broke down over *Tristan and Isolde,* too.

***

When I call her from the car, she answers her phone. *The heavens rejoice!*

And when Emily next speaks, I can hear the smile in her voice, but we have relationship rules and she takes the opportunity to remind me of one of them. "Isn't there *something* you need to say to me?"

I know it's time for me to fall on my sword, because one thing I love about Emmy is her ability to forgive me when I say I'm sorry. "I have been a very naughty girl and I'm so incredibly sorry, so you can spank me hard, as hard as you want to."

She sighs with the utter satisfaction of hearing the official apology. "Fine, then. And isn't there one more thing you need to ask me?"

I only have to think about this for a split second. "What does stupi-bog-gled mean?" I ask obediently.

Emily doesn't try to hide her giggle of glee. "Stupified, combined with mind-boggled. You likey?"

"I love it, and let me explain why I'm bailing on the list...."

"You don't have to spell it out for me. I know that life isn't easy for Jas-per. He practically raises his younger sister. I don't think I've ever seen him anywhere after school without her."

"But Em, at lunch today, Jazz bailed on me."

"He what? Stupi-boggled BFF here!"

"The list worked. He admitted he fell for me."

"So where does the 'Jazz dumping you' part come in?"

I sigh, long and loud. "The Plan worked too well. He thinks I am all of those things I acted like. Jazz thinks I'm beautiful and perpetually smiling and—"

"Well, you are."

"Emmy, he thinks I am hard to get and too busy to spend time with him and too complicated for a simple guy like him."

"Oh."

112

Neither of us says anything for a few long seconds.

"I get why you're bailing on the plan, Channy."

"Thanks, Em. And thanks a lot for being so cool about this." She *is* so cool. "But I'm not a one-trick pony—I think I can do friendship with him."

"I'm sure you can. You're the best friend I've ever had, I know that much. Not to be sappy… but Jazz will be lucky to have you as a bro."

"I seriously just melted."

"I adore you, Channy. Call me after dinner."

***

The goddamn List for the freaking stupid no good Plan.
What was I thinking when I made this the motto of my life?
I sit at the desk in my room, ready to delete the documents that messed up my life beyond repair. But this annoying voice in the back of my head reminds me that the two "lame" items I'd skipped, numbers nine and ten, might actually have been important. I decide I will look at the asinine List one more time, and see what I missed.

9. Friendship is key. Love is about being true friends with each other

How could I have thought that number nine wasn't important? Cuz now it's clear to me—friendship is the basis of all meaningful relationships. I am stupi-boggled at how far off base I've been when it comes to Jazz, and that's really saying a lot, because normally I don't even acknowledge baseball analogies.

10. Always be yourself—this is the most important of all

Gotta say, Dr. Whatever-your-name-is who wrote the online article—I kinda wish you'd placed this golden nugget of wisdom at number *one* on the list instead of at number *ten*.

Like, *duh!*

But maybe, if I make the decision to give the author of "Ten Scientifically Proven Ways to Make a Man Fall in Love With You" the benefit of the doubt, I can make myself believe that she was saving the best for last.

* if you are being someone you are not, you are setting your-

self up to fail—you can't hold up an illusion of perfection forever

Yeah, this little gem would've been nice to know back when I was smiling until my lip muscles burned and my eyes watered.

* keep in mind that he wants to know the real you—the girl with all of the flaws

Well, I have no shortage of flaws, seeing as I can't decide between girl and boy, so I wouldn't have disappointed him here.

* stay true to yourself—only this will win you the prize you want

What is it they always say about hindsight?

Chapter 24
Calm Before the Storm

The next few days drag by. I'd like to say I've been focused mainly on my deep thankfulness for my friendships with Jazz and Em, but without the challenge of trying to make Jazz fall in love with me, my mind keeps on wandering in the direction of my biggest dooza-palooza. Which can be summed up in a single question.

At the very core of my being, am I male or female?

I know what my body is.

I know what my sexuality is.

I just don't know what *I* am.

I *do*, however, know what I like.

I like silky soft purple things on certain days and I like skinny jeans and funny hoodies on other days. I like the way eyeliner looks and Chapstick feels. I like to be creative with my hair and to make colorful comforters to cover my furniture. At times I like to be strong and respected and admired, but other times I want to be protected and fussed over and held in strong arms. And I always like to be a good friend.

I don't know what the word is for what I am.

I don't really want to figure it out, but I'm starting to think I have to.

***

And so I just walk right to his lunch table. No lurking around three tables away to see if he can sense my impending arrival, no grinning my ass off, no seductive lip motions. Just Chance sitting down and saying, "Hi, guys", to Jazz, Tessa, and Kyle. This is what friends do.

The taste of friendship is admittedly bittersweet, but I'm strong enough to deal with it.

"Dude, I was hoping you'd come by." Jazz's smile is what you might call pained. Maybe mere friendship doesn't taste too good to him either. "But I'm gonna have to eat fast and then start my English homework. Gotta write an essay I never passed in when I was absent—and I sure suck at essays." He looks down at his lunch tray. "Want a carrot stick or two?"

I picture a skinny strand of carrot sticking out from between my two front teeth and I almost refuse his offer. But then, I think, *Jazz and I are friends and I'm gonna have myself a damned carrot stick.* I reach onto his plate and grab one. "Thanks, Jazz."

He pushes his plate closer to me, and then smiles in that way I like. "Sure thing." I smile back and it's a real smile cuz he's so generous, not an I-dare-you-to-fall-in-love-with-me smile cuz he's so hot. And I don't even try to figure out if the smile reached my eyes. *Just saying.*

"How did Yolo's project on wild horses turn out?"

"Super awesome. She told me to send you a huge thank you for the help."

"Tell her 'huge you're welcome'."

Jazz chuckles. "Cool. I will. Or maybe you wanna tell her yourself, like, say, on Saturday. At the mall. Jo's going to a birthday party at Build-a-Bear Workshop, and so I'm gonna be hangin' out at the mall all afternoon."

"I'd love to hang out with you at the mall." *Be yourself, Chance.* "You may not be able to drag me out of Hot Topic, though." Looks like I'm now a slave to fashion rather than to the The List.

Jazz tilts his head back and laughs heartily, in just the way I'd hoped for when I told him the magic dog joke a few days ago. "You're such a sweetheart, Chance. And if that's where you get all of your nice jeans, you can stay in Hot Topic for as long as you like. 'Kay?"

Huh? Me? Such a sweetheart? Nice jeans? Huh? All I did was tell him the truth.

As soon as he finishes his lunch, I swipe his tray, and say, "Time for your English essay. I'll get rid of this for you." And when I get back from discarding his trash, he's staring at me in a different way than ever before.

"Thanks, man."

"So what's this essay about, anyway, Jazz? Maybe I can help you out."

I'm the recipient of another kick-ass smile before he slides his paper toward me to show me his progress. If this is friendship with Jazz Donahue, I guess it's not too bad.

And if friendship is all I can have with him, I'm gonna make the most of it.

Can I get an 'Amen'?

Chapter 25
True to Myself

So *maybe* their skinny jeans fit my ass just right, but *maybe* I've discovered I can't get enough of Hot Topic hoodies. And *maybe* Jazz has to forcibly drag me out of the store after I've been in there for an hour and a half.

But *maybe* to my own self I'm finally being true. And *maybe* it's a huge relief.

We laugh all the way to Julio's Pizza at the other end of the mall where we indulge in a large mushroom and pepperoni, my treat. We talk about boring shit—favorite movies, plans for after high school graduation, life's most embarrassing moments (mine, "The Gummy Bear Incident", wins the prize for most humiliating)—and, I'm proud to say, the whole time I sit across from Jazz in the small booth in the cozy back corner of the restaurant, I don't bat my eyelashes once.

That's what I said—*not once!*

At the end of our not-a-date-and-I-don't-wish-it-was-one, Jazz and I sit on the bench across from Build-a-Bear Workshop where we can see Yolo putting the finishing touches on what looks like a My Little Pony stuffed animal, and we're quiet. And it isn't awkward silence. Just normal quiet. Which isn't at all normal for me.

Finally, Jazz says, "Today was so fun."

"It was sick."

I haven't seen one of those baffled glances from Jazz all day, until now.

"It means awesome. Sick means awesome, Jazz."

"Um… but awesome doesn't mean sick, right?"

I shake my head and try not to smile. "No. Awesome means awesome."

Jazz turns around on the bench so he's sitting sideways, looking right at me, and suddenly all I can see are those endlessly deep brown eyes. So soft and open and honest—and I look away because I'm trying to see him as my friend and nothing else. But when he's looking at me this way, I will admit, I see much more.

"Then, you're awesome." He touches my chin to make me look him in the eyes again. "Chance, I think you're awesome."

OMG, I'm gonna spring a leak! Right here, in the middle of the mall— beside the beautifully painted indoor carousel, across from a teddy bear construction zone, and two doors down from a lady's underwear store that I've always secretly wanted to explore—I start to cry.

"Not sick, Chance—*awesome.* Like the real thing kinda awesome." I

117

reach into my Hot Topic bag and pull out one sleeve of my brand-new Buzz Lightyear sweatshirt and use it to wipe my eyes. "You always look so nice and you're funny and never boring, but what I like best is that I can talk to ya real good."

I'm speechless, which is rarer than a sighting of a brown booby bird in Maine. This is just too much. And I can't do this because… because he says I'm awesome, not sick….

"I forgot I have to meet Emily… for a thing at… this place I've got to be at… and I'm late for it." I jump up off that bench like I've been poked in the ass with a glitter-gelled spike of orange hair, and bolt toward my car.

***

When I wake up the next morning, there's a text from Jazz on my phone. *"PLZ meet me & Jo @ Centennial Park by the swing set @ 2. Wear a jacket over ur hoodie, gonna B cold. K?"*

I'm still a freaked-out by what happened between us at the mall yesterday. And I haven't yet been debriefed by Emmy, which is kinda mandatorbs. But friends meet friends at parks, right?

#platonicrealness

This is really no big deal.

I text him back. "K"

Chapter 26
#relationshiprealness

Jazz is right—it's totes cold and windy. He's already pushing Yolo on the swing set when I get there.

"Hi Chance!" Yolo sees me first. "Look and see how high I can go!"

Jazz turns around and offers that smile I like. "Hey—I been waitin' for ya."

"Well, here I am."

"You ran out when I was talking to you yesterday." He doesn't seem angry; he just keeps on pushing Yolo's swing.

"Oh, puh-lease…." I wave him off. "I just remembered I had a previous engagement, that's all."

"Right."

He pushes Yolo one more time and she shouts, "Gonna go to the jungle gym next, you guys." Yolo scuffs her sneakers on the cold dirt until she comes to a stop and then she hops off the swing and skips toward the jungle gym.

Jazz's voice is low and serious when he says, "I was about to tell you something real important when you bolted yesterday."

We both watch his sister trot across the park.

"Let's sit down on the bench over there," he suggests.

And so we walk to the bench closest to the jungle gym and sit down beside each other. It's damned cold and I'm very thankful that I do not have a pocketful of damp honeyed paper pressed against my ass.

"See, what I was gonna tell you, is that you're kinda like everything I wanna be with, all wrapped up in one package."

Well, Jazz is certainly taking the direct approach today. I open my mouth to speak but I can't formulate my thoughts into words. Yes, I'm stupi-boggled.

"You got softer parts—folks may say like a girl—y' know, like how you're about to cry *right now,* and how you like to look pretty and smell real good. But there's another part of you that's all dude, like the way we can really talk so easy together. And because of that I feel comfortable with you."

I manage to overcome my rare speechlessness to protest. "But that's the problem with me, Jazz—can't you see?"

"I don't see a problem."

"Haven't you noticed how… how *different* I am from everybody else?"

He actually takes my hand in his big work-roughened palm. "Course I have."

"I've got no box that I fit into. No single label like a *boy* or a *girl*—I'm stuck in the middle!"

"So what? Why do you need a stupid label?"

"So that I fit in. I don't fit in as a boy or as a—" I stop abruptly. There's no way I'm gonna spill my guts to this guy I'm just learning to trust.

Jazz leans toward me and takes my other hand in his. He doesn't look around to see who might be watching two boys get busy on a park bench. He just keeps staring right at me. "You aren't a typical guy... that's true. But you aren't a total girl, or I wouldn't be sitting here holding your hands like this."

Squeeeee!!!! Jazz is totes gay! Maybe I squeal out loud. It's ain't a crime.

"I'm different, too, Chance. We all got struggles."

He *is* different, and I'm reminded that Emily once said something along the lines of "he's not the sharpest knife in the drawer". But *I* see Jazz as still water, and I know that he runs very deep. Metaphorically, that is.

How does Jazz see me?

"Your way of being—all sassy and bold, and then kind and helpful, and then all super soft and sweet, lots of times funny, and always so pretty—it makes you Chance. So don't change and be all one way or the other, 'kay? You don't have to go into a box. At least, don't go climbing into one of those boxes on account of me."

I release a fret-liberato sigh. Knowing that Jazz doesn't question my gender status kinda relaxes me and makes me feel like maybe I'm fab just where I am—straddling two boxes, one with a "boy" label and one that says "girl". But he was right on the money a couple of minutes ago when he said I was about to cry. Cuz I'm totes bawling right now. "Hashtag such a cry baby," I croak.

"Nah, you're just you." Jazz pulls a hand from mine and points one finger, and then with it he traces the hot pink words on my black hoodie sweatshirt. "All the good ones *are* gay." He grins as he reads the words aloud.

I smile through my tears and it reaches all the way to my eyes, which is a detail that The List for The Plan recommends, but I don't give a crap.

"Take a chance on me, Chance, 'kay?" His words are cheesy enough to choke a large mammal, but they're also super sweet.

I sniff. "Kkkk."

That's when he takes me into his big strong arms—in the park, by the freaking jungle gym, with his sister tugging on his arm.

"Are you guys boyfriends now?" she asks, plain as day. I try to wiggle out of Jazz's arms to avoid a major PDA in front of her.

But Jazz holds on to me fast. "I sure hope so, JoJo."

"Eh? Wha'?" Embarrassingly, I don't just think that.

"He wants you to be his boyfriend, Chance. It's all he ever talks about with Mommy and me at home." Jazz releases just enough to allow me to look at his sister. She's wearing a bright pink flowered ski jacket (want), slightly bent over, with her hands planted on her hips. And to complete the picture, she's rolling her eyes. "Please just say yes to him. Give me and Mommy some peace."

I'm still rather incoherent. "I... not in a box... no label, whatsoever... and I'm genderqueer... or maybe it's fluid.... I don't know which... and... did two love spells... and...."

"But are ya into me?" Jazz asks.

"God, yes!"

"Then we're good to go, huh?" After weeks of manipulation, all it takes is a small dose of honesty and "then we're good to go" for Jazz and me to be boyfriends. He stands, pulling me up with him. "Come on, I wanna bring my sister and my boyfriend for a frozen yogurt on our way home at The Brain Freeze." And then he takes my hand in his, as in, *we're walking across the park holding hands!*

"Jasper, after frozen yogurt, can Chance come to our house and watch a movie?"

Jazz squeezes my hand and says softly to his sister, "I'm kinda countin' on it."

"Wait! I need to take a selfie of us holding hands to send Emily. She's going to want proof when I tell her we hooked up."

"Nah, don't do that. Invite her to meet us at The Brain Freeze instead, and we can show her this." And that's when it happens—Jazz leans in and kisses me. It's honest and sweet, just like his smile. Just like him. "Let's surprise Emily. Don't ya think we should be mysterious?"

I'm still reeling from my first ever kiss. And Jazz's suggestion that we be mysterious reminds me of the online article. *Be a little mysterious*—that's number six on The List, I think... but then I let the whole list and the plan and all of the love spells fall out of my brain onto the frozen grass.

In fact, we step on them as we walk away.

Glossary- in no particular order (totes randatorbs)

Totes= totally
Randatorbs= random
Werk #1= to try very hard
Werk #2= a declaration of support
Werk #3= a goal has been met
Smi-zee= happy to the point of gleeful
Yaaasss= yes times ten
Mandatorbs= mandatory
Adorbs= adorable
Pie-stroll= something that is easy to do, even easier than a cakewalk
Fucker-nelly= extremely
Dooza-palooza= a humongous problem
Suck-ola= stinks, sucks, not good
Poopatude= a nasty attitude
Fret-liberato= relieved
Stupi-boggled= stupefied combined with mind-boggled
Yapper-halt= shut up
Moi= me but more glamorous
Curified= curious combined with horrified
Ratchet= a girl who thinks she is eye candy but isn't
'Rents= parents
Smexy= witty intelligence combined with spicy hotness
Laaaaove= love times ten
Sha-blam= Bam!
Juilliard-Em-mania= emotional backlash suffered by Emily with regard to unwanted discussion of Juilliard college entrance essay
Probs= probably
Libes= library
Sick= awesome
Sickening= over the top awesomeness
K, kk, kkkk= okay
Okaaaaay= okay
B= bitch, but in a playful, positive way
Resting Bitch Face= face of a person who naturally looks mean when expressionless

Mia Kerick

is the mother of four exceptional children—all named after saints—and five non-pedigreed cats—all named after the next best thing to saints, Boston Red Sox players. Her husband of twenty-two years has been told by many that he has the patience of Job, but don't ask Mia about that, as it is a sensitive subject.

Mia focuses her stories on the emotional growth of troubled young people and their relationships, and she believes that physical intimacy has a place in a love story, but not until it is firmly established as a love story. As a teen, Mia filled spiral-bound notebooks with romantic tales of tortured heroes (most of whom happened to strongly resemble lead vocalists of 1980s big-hair bands) and stuffed them under her mattress for safekeeping.

She is thankful to CoolDudes Publishing, Dreamspinner Press, Harmony Ink Press, and CreateSpace for providing her with alternate places to stash her stories.

Mia is a social liberal and cheers for each and every victory made in the name of human rights, especially marital equality. Her only major regret: never having taken typing or computer class in school, destining her to a life consumed with two-fingered pecking and constant prayer to the Gods of Technology.

Books by Mia Kerick

Published by Dreamspinner Press
Beggars and Choosers
Unfinished Business
A Package Deal
Out of Hiding
Random Acts
Here Without You

Published by Harmony Ink Press
Intervention
Not Broken, Just Bent
The Red Sheet
Us Three

Published by CoolDudes Publishing
Inclination

Published by Mia Kerick
Come To My Window

CPSIA information can be obtained at www.ICGtesting.com
Printed in the USA
LVOW01s1421130815

449997LV00024B/519/P